BILLY BUDD, SAILOR

BILLY BUDD,
SAILOR

Herman Melville

Supplementary material written by Kathleen Helal
Series edited by Cynthia Brantley Johnson

POCKET BOOKS
NEW YORK LONDON TORONTO SYDNEY

POCKET BOOKS, a division of Simon & Schuster, Inc.
1230 Avenue of the Americas, New York, NY 10020

This book is a work of fiction. Names, characters, places, and incidents are products of the author's imagination or are used fictitiously. Any resemblance to actual events or locales or persons, living or dead, is entirely coincidental.

ISBN-13: 978-1-4165-2372-7
ISBN-10:   1-4165-2372-3

This Pocket Books paperback edition August 2006

10 9 8 7 6 5 4 3 2 1

POCKET and colophon are registered trademarks of Simon & Schuster, Inc.

Cover art by Marco Ventura

Manufactured in the United States of America

For information regarding special discounts for bulk purchases, please contact Simon & Schuster Special Sales at 1-800-456-6798 or business@simonandschuster.com.

CONTENTS

INTRODUCTION

Billy Budd, Sailor:
MURDER, MUTINY, AND METAPHYSICS

Herman Melville's *Billy Budd* presents a dilemma without resolution: How do we make legal exceptions and still maintain order? On the surface, the plot is about the ethics of murder and the possibility of mutiny, but the narrative also asks metaphysical questions: Can murder be justified? When is mutiny defensible? What is the nature of evil? How can we know the truth of an event?

The action in *Billy Budd* takes place in the summer of 1797, a period of mutiny and revolt on both a large and a small scale. Both the American and the French revolutions transpired near the end of the eighteenth century, and those repressed by the old European regimes began to see that changing the power structure was actually possible. Some of the particulars of the plot are drawn from an actual mutiny on a British ship in 1842, an event that was revisited in popular magazines while Melville was writing and revising the story. What seems to intrigue Melville most in the tale he creates is the historical authority. Within the text, Melville presents competing versions of the story—the story itself, a naval chronicle, and a poem—each of which only partially reveals the "real" story.

Billy Budd is made even more mysterious by its own fragmented publication history. Written in the late 1880s, almost finished at the time of Melville's death in 1891, the text was published in one version in 1924 and in quite another in 1962. Critics have approached the work from completely divergent angles, so there is little consensus as to the story's meaning or Melville's intentions. The answers to the questions Melville raises are as enigmatic as the interpretations are irreconcilable. But perhaps this was Melville's intent all along—to call into question an author's authority, to make readers feel that the gap between what they are shown by writers and historians and "the truth" may be wider than they realized.

The Life and Work of Herman Melville

Herman Melville explored profound conflicts among nature, society, and humanity through the vehicle of his past experiences at sea in his epic tales, most notably in *Moby-Dick* (1851). He was born in New York City on August 1, 1819, to Allan Melvill and Maria Melvill, who changed the family name when her husband died. The third of eight children, Herman was considered intellectually slow, especially after an infection of scarlet fever left him partially blind. The family was financially secure until his father's import business failed in 1830, and they were forced to move to Albany, where Allan died two years later. His father's death signaled not only the end of Melville's childhood but also the end of his affluent and privileged life.

So at the age of twelve, Melville went to work at various jobs: farmhand, clerk, teacher. In 1841 he joined the crew of the whaling ship *Acushnet*. His experience as a sailor would later inspire him to write some of the greatest fiction in American literature. On the series of voyages from 1841 to 1844, Melville traveled the Pacific, even living briefly with cannibals in the Marquesas Islands. After eighteen months aboard the *Acushnet* from 1841 to 1842, he escaped with his shipmate Richard Tobias Greene to stay briefly with the Typees, a native tribe on the island of Nukahiva. Melville departed Nukahiva on the *Lucy Ann*, an Australian whaler, where he participated in a nonviolent mutiny that landed him in a Tahitian jail. From Tahiti, he traveled to Maui on the whaler *Charles and Henry*. After spending three months in Hawaii, he signed up to serve as a military seaman on the USS *United States*, the ship that would transport him back to Boston a year and a half later in 1844.

Shortly after returning to America, Melville began revisiting his own experiences while reading narratives from other sea travelers to prepare to write his own fiction. His interaction with the Marquesan natives led him to write his first novel, *Typee: A Peep at Polynesian Life* (1846), an innovative and controversial celebration of native culture and a critique of the Christian missionary misinterpretations of it. The novel was so popular that Melville wrote a sequel, *Omoo: A Narrative of Adventures in the South Seas* (1847), which proved to be equally successful. In 1847, he married Elizabeth Shaw, whose father, Lemuel Shaw, was chief justice of the Massachusetts Supreme Court. Shortly after the marriage, he began writing *Mardi: And a Voyage Thither* (1849), a novel that began as another adventure narrative but ended up as a complex literary work that alienated readers of his earlier novels. Looking for another popular success, Melville returned to a more conventional style in his next two works, *Redburn: His First Voyage* (1849) and *White-Jacket: The World in a Man-of-War* (1850). His next novel, *Moby-Dick; or, The Whale* (1851), would solidify his reputation as a writer and would, in time, be judged his greatest book.

Nothing Melville published after *Moby-Dick* seemed to compare to the widely recognized masterpiece. *Pierre; or, The Ambiguities* (1852) disrupted readers' expectations and disappointed critics. The novella *Israel Potter: His Fifty Years of Exile* (1855), drawn from the memoirs of an American Revolutionary War veteran, was only moderately successful. Some of the short stories he compiled in *The Piazza Tales* (1856), including "Bartleby the Scrivener" and "Benito Cereno," are now recognized as classics, but they were not celebrated at the time of their publication. His last novel, *The Confidence-Man: His Masquerade* (1857), generated such a negative critical reception that Melville stopped writing fiction altogether for almost thirty years. After lecturing and traveling for a few years, he returned to New York and accepted a post as district inspector of customs in 1866, a job he held until his retirement two decades later. During this period, both of Melville's sons died: Malcolm committed suicide in 1867, and Stanwix died of a fever in 1886 in San Francisco. Though he was not writing fiction anymore, Melville did write poetry and published the two-volume epic *Clarel: A Poem and Pilgrimage in the Holy Land* in 1876. The last two works published during his lifetime were the poetic collections *John Marr and Other Sailors* (1888), which contains the poem "Billy in the Darbies," and *Timoleon* (1891).

When he died of a heart attack on September 28, 1891, it was said that most people thought he had died long before. But critics would revive his reputation in the 1920s, especially with the posthumous publication of a text no one knew existed, *Billy Budd*. Since this revival, Melville has become known as one of the greatest American writers.

Historical and Literary Context of *Billy Budd*

The Threat of Mutiny

Melville stages his drama in the summer of 1797, a time during which many British naval officers were anxious about the possibility of mutiny. Three of the most famous mutinies in British history took place during the late eighteenth century; two of them occurred in 1797. The most famous of these was the mutiny on the HMS *Bounty* in 1789, when the autocratic Lieutenant William Bligh was forced off his ship onto a small boat with eighteen other men. In April of 1797, British seamen, outraged at their living conditions at sea and indignant about their status as impressed men, orchestrated a mutiny on a ship at Spithead, the strategically significant strait of the English Channel. They were successful in negotiating better pay and improved living conditions, as some senior British officers agreed that changes were necessary. Even Admiral Nelson, the heroic commander to whom Captain Vere is compared, praised the mutineers for rebelling. In a letter to the Duke of Clarence on May 26, 1797, he wrote: "To us who see the whole at once we must think that for a Mutiny which I fear I must call it having no other name, that it has been the most Manly thing I ever heard of, and does the British Sailor infinite honor."

Less than a month later, mutineers took over another British ship and sailed to Nore, a frequently used sandbank at the opening of the Thames River. The narrator describes the Nore mutiny as "a demonstration more menacing to England than the contemporary manifestoes and conquering and proselyting armies" of France, Britain's primary enemy. These mutinies at Spithead and Nore make Captain Vere paranoid that insurrection on his ship, the *Bellipotent*, is imminent.

Melville also explicitly refers to another mutiny that took place almost half a century later. In the chapter in which Captain Vere and his drumhead court try Billy, the narrator says the members of the court "were brought to something more or less akin to that harassed frame of mind which in the year 1842 actuated the commander of the brig-of-war USS *Somers* to resolve." Though the narrator acknowledges that the situation was different, the officers felt a similar sense of urgency. Captain Alexander Slidell Mackenzie presided over the trial and the hanging of three men who were found guilty of plotting mutiny on the USS *Somers*. Popular magazine articles surfacing during the time Melville was writing *Billy Budd* reminded audiences of the complexities and mysteries of the *Somers* mutiny. Had *Billy Budd* been published in 1891, audiences would have been familiar with this mutiny, and the injustice of Budd's fate would have resonated with them.

Impressment and Cultural Slavery

There is unrest on board the *Bellipotent* not only because of the threat of mutiny, but also because many of the men have been forced into military service, or *impressed*. This brutal practice was carried out regularly by "press gangs," or groups of men with orders to recruit men by any means necessary, kidnapping them at times, violently disciplining them, and severely restricting their freedom. But impressment was not a controversial issue during Melville's time. Slavery was the topic that dominated political debates during the latter half of the nineteenth century. Melville clearly abhorred the practice of subjugating any human. He suggests not only that impressed men were like slaves, but also that race does not determine identity. Indeed, he introduces his impressed hero by comparing him to a "common sailor so intensely black that he must needs have been a native African of the unadulterated blood of Ham." In this suggestion that the heroic Budd is like the black sailor, who is a descendant of Ham, the biblical figure cursed by Noah in the Old Testament to be a slave, Melville rebels against the conventional belief that people of color are inferior to whites. Though Melville's disgust with racial injustice is not as fully articulated in *Billy Budd* as in some of his other texts, the narrative suggests that both impressment and cultural slavery create conditions that force individuals either to rebel or to join the quest for imperial dominance.

Slow Road to Publication

The literary context for *Billy Budd* is complex, not only because it was not published when it was first written, but also because the version that circulated for almost forty years was the wrong one. The novella was never published during Melville's lifetime, and the original manuscripts reveal not only that the work was not finalized at the time of his death, but also that Melville's wife edited it. Raymond Weaver, who transcribed and published the first edition of this text in 1924, based his title on the words written out on a sheet of paper attached to the manuscript that read "Billy Budd / Foretopman / What befell him / in the year of the / Great Mutiny / &c." What Weaver did not know is that Mrs. Melville wrote these words and made many of the markings, deletions, and additions that appeared on the original manuscripts.

When Harrison Hayford and Merton M. Sealts published their revised version of Melville's text in 1962, they revolutionized the way readers would perceive *Billy Budd*. Hayford and Sealts, who carefully analyzed the original manuscripts at Houghton Library to publish their authoritative text, were able to distinguish Melville's handwriting and used the title he wrote: *Billy Budd, Sailor (An Inside Narrative)*. They also proved earlier claims that the title was originally *Baby Budd, Sailor*, and that the orginal manuscript had neither a preface nor a coda. The Hayford-Sealts text includes a "Reading Text" with notes that aid interpretation of the story, and a "Genetic Text," or a reprint of the manuscript as it was found when Melville died, and highlights corrections and marks made by his wife. The Hayford-Sealts edition has been considered the definitive version of *Billy Budd* since its publication.

CHRONOLOGY OF HERMAN MELVILLE'S LIFE AND WORK

1819: Herman Melville born on August 1 in New York City.

1832: Melville's father, Allan Melvill, dies; Melville drops out of school.

1832–18: Melville works as a clerk in a bank, and then on a farm owned by his uncle.

1835: Works at his brother Gansevoort's store in Albany; enrolls in the Classical School.

1837: Teaches in a country school near Pittsfield.

1839: Signs on to the *St. Lawrence*, a trading ship that takes him from New York to Liverpool and back again.

1841: Sails on the *Acushnet*, a whaler bound for the South Seas.

1842: Jumps ship at Nukahiva in the Marquesas; lives with a Typee tribe for a month.

1842–44: Travels on a number of whalers, including *Lucy Ann* and *Charles and Henry*.

1843: Discharged from the *Charles and Henry* in Lahaina, Hawaii; enlists in American Navy and sails for Boston on the warship USS *United States*.

1844: Arrives in Boston and is discharged from the United States Navy.

1846: Publishes his first book, *Typee: A Peep at Polynesian Life*, based on his experiences in the Marquesas.

1847: Marries Elizabeth Knapp Shaw, daughter of Lemuel Shaw, chief justice of Massachusetts; publishes *Omoo;* moves back to New York City.

1849: Publishes *Mardi*, a work critics call eccentric and difficult, and *Redburn*, a more straightforward adventure tale; first son, Malcolm, is born.

1850: Publishes *White-Jacket*, based on his experiences on the USS *United States;* meets Nathaniel Hawthorne.

1851: Second son, Stanwix, is born; publishes *Moby-Dick*.

1852: Publishes *Pierre; or, The Ambiguities*, a work that left readers questioning his sanity.

1853: First daughter, Elizabeth, born; "Bartleby the Scrivener" published.

1854: Contributes to magazines with installments of "The Encantadas" and *Israel Potter*.

1855: Second daughter, Frances, born; *Israel Potter* and "Benito Cereno" published.

1856: Publishes several of his short stories in *The Piazza Tales;* travels to the Holy Land.

1857: Publishes his last work of prose, titled *The Confidence-Man: His Masquerade*.

1857–60: Lectures unsuccessfully in various cities in America on such topics as "The South Seas" and "Traveling."

1866: Begins a career as a customs inspector; volume of poetry, *Battle-Pieces*, published.

1867: Oldest son, Malcolm, commits suicide at the age of eighteen.

1872: Melville's mother and his brother Allan die.

1876: Publishes *Clarel: A Poem and Pilgrimage in the Holy Land*.

1886: Second son, Stanwix, dies; Melville retires from Custom House.

1888: *John Marr and Other Sailors*, volume of poems published privately; "Billy in the Darbies," poetic genesis of *Billy Budd* is included.

1891: Publishes his last volume of poems, *Timoleon*, and dedicates it to his wife; dies of a heart attack in relative obscurity.

1924: *Billy Budd: Foretopman* is published posthumously and received favorably.

1962: Harrison Hayford and Merton M. Sealts publish *Billy Budd, Sailor (An Inside Narrative)*.

HISTORICAL CONTEXT OF
Billy Budd, Sailor

1789: French Revolution begins; mutiny on the HMS *Bounty*.

1790: British philosopher Edmund Burke argues in *Reflections on the French Revolution* that individual rights should be subordinate to social order.

1791: Thomas Paine counters Burke's argument in *The Rights of Man*, declaring the superiority of natural rights.

1793–94: Reign of Terror in France; more than 30,000 die.

1794: The United States Navy is officially formed; the Jay Treaty between the United States and Britain, an attempt to resolve postrevolutionary issues, fuels controversy about the practice of impressment by failing to address it.

1795: French Directory, an interim regime of five rulers, begins governing France.

1797: The first three ships of the United States Navy, USS *United States*, USS *Constellation*, and USS

Constitution, are launched; mutinies at Spithead and Nore threaten military stability in the British Navy; British Admiral Horatio Nelson loses his arm in a battle for the Spanish island of Tenerife.

1799: Napoléon Bonaparte usurps power of the French government.

1800: Franz Joseph Gall introduces his theory of cranioscopy, or the study of external features of the skull to determine personality, mentality, and morality, a theory his collaborator Johann Spurzheim would later rename phrenology.

1801: The Kingdom of Great Britain and the Kingdom of Ireland merge to form the United Kingdom under King George III.

1802: Scottish engineer William Symington constructs the first functional steamboat.

1805: Admiral Nelson is victorious at Trafalgar, but he dies during the battle.

1815: Allied forces from the United Kingdom, Prussia, Austria, and Russia defeat Napoléon I at Waterloo.

1819: First transatlantic steamship voyage by the USS *Savannah*.

1833: Slavery Abolition Act prohibits slavery in the United Kingdom.

1837: Victoria becomes queen of the United Kingdom and begins a sixty-four-year reign during which the British Empire expands.

1842: On the USS *Somers*, Captain Alexander Slidell Mackenzie hangs three suspected mutineers, including Philip Spencer, son of the secretary of war.

1861–65: United States Civil War.

1886: Workers striking for an eight-hour workday clash with policemen in Chicago's Haymarket Square in what is called the Haymarket Riot; four rioters are hanged.

1888: *American Magazine* revives interest in the *Somers* affair by publishing "The Mutiny on the *Somers*," an article that favors Captain Mackenzie's actions.

1889: Gail Hamilton attacks Captain Mackenzie in "The Murder of Philip Spencer," a fictional series published in *Cosmopolitan Magazine*.

1891: The same month of Melville's death, Congress passes copyright law, for which Melville and other writers lobbied forty years earlier.

Billy Budd, Sailor

(An Inside Narrative)

Dedicated to JACK CHASE, Englishman
Wherever that great heart may now be
Here on Earth or harbored in Paradise
Captain of the Maintop in the year 1843
in the U.S. Frigate *United States*

1

IN THE TIME before steamships, or then more frequently than now, a stroller along the docks of any considerable seaport would occasionally have his attention arrested by a group of bronzed mariners, man-of-war's[1] men or merchant sailors in holiday attire, ashore on liberty. In certain instances they would flank, or like a bodyguard quite surround, some superior figure of their own class, moving along with them like Aldebaran[2] among the lesser lights of his constellation. That signal object was the "Handsome Sailor" of the less prosaic time alike of the military and merchant navies. With no perceptible trace of the vainglorious about him, rather with the offhand unaffectedness of natural regality, he seemed to accept the spontaneous homage of his shipmates.

A somewhat remarkable instance recurs to me. In Liverpool,[3] now half a century ago, I saw under the shadow of the great dingy street-wall of Prince's Dock (an obstruction long since removed) a common sailor so intensely black that he must needs have been a native African of the unadulterate blood of Ham[4]—a symmetric figure much above the average height. The two ends of a gay silk handkerchief thrown loose about the neck danced upon the displayed ebony of his chest, in his ears were big hoops of gold, and a Highland bonnet with a tartan band set off his shapely head. It was a hot noon in July; and his face, lustrous with perspiration, beamed with barbaric good humor. In jovial sallies right and left, his white teeth flashing into view, he rollicked along, the center of a company of his shipmates. These were made up of such an assortment of tribes and complexions as would have well fitted them to be marched up by Anacharsis Cloots[5] before the bar of the first French Assembly as Representatives of the Human Race. At each spontaneous tribute rendered by the wayfarers to this black pagod[6] of a fellow—the tribute of a pause and stare, and less frequently an exclamation—the motley retinue showed that they took that sort of pride in the evoker of it which the Assyrian priests doubtless showed for their grand sculptured Bull when the faithful prostrated themselves.

To return. If in some cases a bit of a nautical Murat[7] in setting forth his person ashore, the Handsome Sailor of the period in question evinced nothing of the dandified Billy-be-Dam, an amusing character all but extinct now, but occasionally to be encountered, and in a form yet more amusing than the original, at the tiller of the boats on the tempestuous Erie Canal or, more likely, vaporing in the groggeries along the towpath. Invariably a proficient in his perilous calling, he was also more or less of a mighty boxer or wrestler. It was strength and beauty. Tales of his prowess were recited. Ashore he was the champion; afloat the spokesman; on every suitable occasion always foremost. Close-reefing topsails in a gale, there he was, astride the weather yardarm-end, foot in the Flemish horse as stirrup, both hands tugging at the earing as at a bridle, in very much the attitude of young Alexander curbing the fiery Bucephalus.[8] A superb figure, tossed up as by the horns of Taurus against the thunderous sky, cheerily hallooing to the strenuous file along the spar.

The moral nature was seldom out of keeping with the physical make. Indeed, except as toned by the former, the comeliness and power, always attractive in masculine conjunction, hardly could have drawn the sort of honest homage the Handsome Sailor in some examples received from his less gifted associates.

Such a cynosure, at least in aspect, and something such too in nature, though with important variations made apparent as the story proceeds, was welkin-eyed Billy Budd—or Baby Budd, as more familiarly, under circumstances hereafter to be given, he at last came to be called—aged twenty-one, a foretopman[9] of the British fleet toward the close of the last decade of the eighteenth century. It was not very long prior to the time of the narration that follows that he had entered the King's service, having been impressed[10] on the Narrow Seas from a homeward-bound English merchantman into a seventy-four outward bound, H.M.S. *Bellipotent*;[11] which ship, as was not unusual in those hurried days, having been obliged to put to sea short of her proper complement of men. Plump upon Billy at first sight in the gangway the boarding officer, Lieutenant Ratcliffe, pounced, even before the merchantman's crew was formally mustered on the quarter-deck for his deliberate inspection.

And him only he elected. For whether it was because the other men when ranged before him showed to ill advantage after Billy, or whether he had some scruples in view of the merchantman's being rather short-handed, however it might be, the officer contented himself with his first spontaneous choice. To the surprise of the ship's company, though much to the lieutenant's satisfaction, Billy made no demur. But, indeed, any demur would have been as idle as the protest of a goldfinch popped into a cage.

Noting this uncomplaining acquiescence, all but cheerful, one might say, the shipmaster turned a surprised glance of silent reproach at the sailor. The shipmaster was one of those worthy mortals found in every vocation, even the humbler ones—the sort of person whom everybody agrees in calling "a respectable man." And—nor so strange to report as it may appear to be—though a ploughman of the troubled waters, lifelong contending with the intractable elements, there was nothing this honest soul at heart loved better than simple peace and quiet. For the rest, he was fifty or thereabouts, a little inclined to corpulence, a prepossessing face, unwhiskered, and of an agreeable color—a rather full face, humanely intelligent in expression. On a fair day with a fair wind and all going well, a certain musical chime in his voice seemed to be the veritable unobstructed outcome of the innermost man. He had much prudence, much conscientiousness, and there were occasions when these virtues were the cause of overmuch disquietude in him. On a passage, so long as his craft was in any proximity to land, no sleep for Captain Graveling. He took to heart those serious responsibilities not so heavily borne by some shipmasters.

Now while Billy Budd was down in the forecastle getting his kit together, the *Bellipotent*'s lieutenant, burly and bluff, nowise disconcerted by Captain Graveling's omitting to proffer the customary hospitalities on an occasion so unwelcome to him, an omission simply caused by preoccupation of thought, unceremoniously invited himself into the cabin, and also to a flask from the spirit locker, a receptacle which his experienced eye instantly discovered. In fact he was one of those sea dogs in whom all the hardship and peril of naval life in the great prolonged wars of his time never impaired the natural instinct for sensuous enjoyment. His duty he always faithfully did; but duty is sometimes a dry obligation, and he was for irrigating its aridity, whensoever possible, with a fertilizing decoction of strong waters. For the cabin's proprietor there was nothing left but to play the part of the enforced host with whatever grace and alacrity were practicable. As necessary adjuncts to the flask, he silently placed tumbler and water jug before the irrepressible guest. But excusing himself from partaking just then, he dismally watched the unembarrassed officer deliberately diluting his grog a little, then tossing it off in three swallows, pushing the empty tumbler away, yet not so far as to be beyond easy reach, at the same time settling himself in his seat and smacking his lips with high satisfaction, looking straight at the host.

These proceedings over, the master broke the silence; and there lurked a rueful reproach in the tone of his voice: "Lieutenant, you are going to take my best man from me, the jewel of 'em."

"Yes, I know," rejoined the other, immediately drawing back the tumbler preliminary to a replenishing. "Yes, I know. Sorry."

"Beg pardon, but you don't understand, Lieutenant. See here, now. Before I shipped that young fellow, my forecastle was a rat-pit of quarrels. It was black times, I tell you, aboard the *Rights* here. I was worried to that degree my pipe had no comfort for me. But Billy came; and it was like a Catholic priest striking peace in an Irish shindy. Not that he preached to them or said or did anything in particular; but a virtue went out of him, sugaring the sour ones. They took to him like hornets to treacle; all but the buffer of the gang, the big shaggy chap with the fire-red whiskers. He indeed, out of envy, perhaps, of the newcomer, and thinking such a "sweet and pleasant fellow," as he mockingly designated him to the others, could hardly have the spirit of a gamecock, must needs bestir himself in trying to get up an ugly row with him. Billy forebore with him and reasoned with him in a pleasant way—he is something like myself, Lieutenant, to whom aught like a quarrel is hateful—but nothing served. So, in the second dogwatch one day, the Red Whiskers in presence of the others, under pretense of showing Billy just whence a sirloin steak was cut—for the fellow had once been a butcher—insultingly gave him a dig under the ribs. Quick as lightning Billy let fly his arm. I dare say he never meant to do quite as much as he did, but anyhow he gave the burly fool a terrible drubbing. It took about half a minute, I should think. And, lord bless you, the lubber was astonished at the celerity. And will you believe it, Lieutenant, the Red Whiskers now really loves Billy—loves him, or is the biggest hypocrite that ever I heard of. But they all love him. Some of 'em do his washing, darn his old trousers for him; the carpenter is at odd times making a pretty little chest of drawers for him. Anybody will do anything for Billy Budd; and it's the

happy family here. But now, Lieutenant, if that young
fellow goes—I know how it will be aboard the *Rights*.
Not again very soon shall I, coming up from dinner, lean
over the capstan smoking a quiet pipe—no, not very
soon again, I think. Ay, Lieutenant, you are going to take
away the jewel of 'em; you are going to take away my
peacemaker!" And with that the good soul had really
some ado in checking a rising sob.

"Well," said the lieutenant, who had listened with
amused interest to all this and now was waxing merry
with his tipple; "well, blessed are the peacemakers,
especially the fighting peacemakers. And such are the
seventy-four beauties some of which you see poking
their noses out of the portholes of yonder warship lying
to for me," pointing through the cabin window at the
Bellipotent. "But courage! Don't look so downhearted,
man. Why, I pledge you in advance the royal approba-
tion. Rest assured that His Majesty will be delighted to
know that in a time when his hardtack is not sought for
by sailors with such avidity as should be, a time also
when some shipmasters privily resent the borrowing
from them a tar or two for the service; His Majesty, I say,
will be delighted to learn that *one* shipmaster at least
cheerfully surrenders to the King the flower of his flock,
a sailor who with equal loyalty makes no dissent.—But
where's my beauty? Ah," looking through the cabin's
open door, "here he comes; and, by Jove, lugging along
his chest—Apollo with his portmanteau!—My man,"
stepping out to him, "you can't take that big box aboard a
warship. The boxes there are mostly shot boxes. Put your
duds in a bag, lad. Boot and saddle for the cavalryman,
bag and hammock for the man-of-war's man."

The transfer from chest to bag was made. And, after

seeing his man into the cutter and then following him
down, the lieutenant pushed off from the *Rights-of-
Man.*[12] That was the merchant ship's name, though by
her master and crew abbreviated in sailor fashion into
the *Rights.* The hard-headed Dundee owner was a
staunch admirer of Thomas Paine, whose book in rejoin-
der to Burke's arraignment of the French Revolution had
then been published for some time and had gone everywhere. In christening his vessel after the title of Paine's
volume the man of Dundee was something like his contemporary shipowner, Stephen Girard of Philadelphia,
whose sympathies, alike with his native land and its lib-
eral philosophers, he evinced by naming his ships after
Voltaire, Diderot,[13] and so forth.

But now, when the boat swept under the merchantman's stern, and officer and oarsmen were noting—some
bitterly and others with a grin—the name emblazoned
there; just then it was that the new recruit jumped up
from the bow where the coxswain had directed him to
sit, and waving hat to his silent shipmates sorrowfully
looking over at him from the taffrail, bade the lads a genial good-bye. Then, making a salutation as to the ship
herself, "And good-bye to you too, old *Rights-of-Man.*"

"Down, sir!" roared the lieutenant, instantly assuming
all the rigor of his rank, though with difficulty repressing
a smile.

To be sure, Billy's action was a terrible breach of naval
decorum. But in that decorum he had never been instructed; in consideration of which the lieutenant would
hardly have been so energetic in reproof but for the concluding farewell to the ship. This he rather took as meant
to convey a covert sally on the new recruit's part, a sly
slur at impressment in general, and that of himself in

especial. And yet, more likely, if satire it was in effect, it was hardly so by intention, for Billy, though happily endowed with the gaiety of high health, youth, and a free heart, was yet by no means of a satirical turn. The will to it and the sinister dexterity were alike wanting. To deal in double meanings and insinuations of any sort was quite foreign to his nature.

As to his enforced enlistment, that he seemed to take pretty much as he was wont to take any vicissitude of weather. Like the animals, though no philosopher, he was, without knowing it, practically a fatalist. And it may be that he rather liked this adventurous turn in his affairs, which promised an opening into novel scenes and martial excitements.

Aboard the *Bellipotent* our merchant sailor was forthwith rated as an able seaman and assigned to the starboard watch of the foretop. He was soon at home in the service, not at all disliked for his unpretentious good looks and a sort of genial happy-go-lucky air. No merrier man in his mess: in marked contrast to certain other individuals included like himself among the impressed portion of the ship's company; for these when not actively employed were sometimes, and more particularly in the last dogwatch when the drawing near of twilight induced revery, apt to fall into a saddish mood which in some partook of sullenness. But they were not so young as our foretopman, and no few of them must have known a hearth of some sort, others may have had wives and children left, too probably, in uncertain circumstances, and hardly any but must have had acknowledged kith and kin, while for Billy, as will shortly be seen, his entire family was practically invested in himself.

2

Though our new-made foretopman was well received in the top and on the gun decks, hardly here was he that cynosure he had previously been among those minor ship's companies of the merchant marine, with which companies only had he hitherto consorted.

He was young, and despite his all but fully developed frame, in aspect looked even younger than he really was, owing to a lingering adolescent expression in the as yet smooth face all but feminine in purity of natural complexion but where, thanks to his seagoing, the lily was quite suppressed and the rose had some ado visibly to flush through the tan.

To one essentially such a novice in the complexities of factitious life, the abrupt transition from his former and simpler sphere to the ampler and more knowing world of a great warship; this might well have abashed him had there been any conceit or vanity in his composition. Among her miscellaneous multitude, the *Bellipotent* mustered several individuals who however inferior in

grade were of no common natural stamp, sailors more
signally susceptive of that air which continuous martial
discipline and repeated presence in battle can in some
degree impart even to the average man. As the Handsome Sailor, Billy Budd's position aboard the seventy-four
was something analogous to that of a rustic beauty trans-
planted from the provinces and brought into competition
with the highborn dames of the court. But this change of
circumstances he scarce noted. As little did he observe
that something about him provoked an ambiguous smile
in one or two harder faces among the bluejackets.[1] Nor
less unaware was he of the peculiar favorable effect his
person and demeanor had upon the more intelligent
gentlemen of the quarter-deck. Nor could this well have
been otherwise. Cast in a mold peculiar to the finest
physical examples of those Englishmen in whom the
Saxon strain would seem not at all to partake of any Nor-
man or other admixture, he showed in face that humane
look of reposeful good nature which the Greek sculptor
in some instances gave to his heroic strong man, Hercules.[2] But this again was subtly modified by another and
pervasive quality. The ear, small and shapely, the arch of
the foot, the curve in mouth and nostril, even the in-
durated hand dyed to the orange-tawny of the toucan's
bill, a hand telling alike of the halyards[3] and tar bucket;
but, above all, something in the mobile expression, and
every chance attitude and movement, something suggestive of a mother eminently favored by Love and the
Graces; all this strangely indicated a lineage in direct con-
tradiction to his lot. The mysteriousness here became less
mysterious through a matter of fact elicited when Billy at
the capstan was being formally mustered into the service.
Asked by the officer, a small, brisk little gentleman as it

chanced, among other questions, his place of birth, he replied, "Please, sir, I don't know."

"Don't know where you were born? Who was your father?"

"God knows, sir."

Struck by the straightforward simplicity of these replies, the officer next asked, "Do you know anything about your beginning?"

"No, sir. But I have heard that I was found in a pretty silk-lined basket hanging one morning from the knocker of a good man's door in Bristol."

"*Found,* say you? Well," throwing back his head and looking up and down the new recruit; "well, it turns out to have been a pretty good find. Hope they'll find some more like you, my man; the fleet sadly needs them."

Yes, Billy Budd was a foundling, a presumable by-blow, and, evidently, no ignoble one. Noble descent was as evident in him as in a blood horse.

For the rest, with little or no sharpness of faculty or any trace of the wisdom of the serpent, nor yet quite a dove, he possessed that kind and degree of intelligence going along with the unconventional rectitude of a sound human creature, one to whom not yet has been proffered the questionable apple of knowledge. He was illiterate; he could not read, but he could sing, and like the illiterate nightingale was sometimes the composer of his own song.

Of self-consciousness he seemed to have little or none, or about as much as we may reasonably impute to a dog of Saint Bernard's breed.

Habitually living with the elements and knowing little more of the land than as a beach, or, rather, that portion of the terraqueous globe providentially set apart for dance-houses, doxies, and tapsters, in short what sailors call a "fiddler's green," his simple nature remained unsophisticated by those moral obliquities which are not in every case incompatible with that manufacturable thing known as respectability. But are sailors, frequenters of fiddlers' greens, without vices? No; but less often than with landsmen do their vices, so called, partake of crookedness of heart, seeming less to proceed from viciousness than exuberance of vitality after long constraint: frank manifestations in accordance with natural law. By his original constitution aided by the co-operating influences of his lot, Billy in many respects was little more than a sort of upright barbarian, much such perhaps as Adam[4] presumably might have been ere the urbane Serpent wriggled himself into his company.

And here be it submitted that apparently going to corroborate the doctrine of man's Fall,[5] a doctrine now popularly ignored, it is observable that where certain virtues pristine and unadulterate peculiarly characterize anybody in the external uniform of civilization, they will upon scrutiny seem not to be derived from custom or convention, but rather to be out of keeping with these, as if indeed exceptionally transmitted from a period prior to Cain's city and citified man.[6] The character marked by such qualities has to an unvitiated taste an untampered-with flavor like that of berries, while the man thoroughly civilized, even in a fair specimen of the breed, has to the same moral palate a questionable smack as of a compounded wine. To any stray inheritor of these primitive qualities found, like Caspar Hauser,[7] wandering dazed in any Christian capital of our time, the good-natured poet's famous invocation, near two thousand years ago, of the good rustic out of his latitude in the Rome of the Caesars, still appropriately holds:

> Honest and poor, faithful in word and thought,
> What hath thee, Fabian, to the city brought?[8]

Though our Handsome Sailor had as much of masculine beauty as one can expect anywhere to see; nevertheless, like the beautiful woman in one of Hawthorne's minor tales, there was just one thing amiss in him. No visible blemish indeed, as with the lady; no, but an occasional liability to a vocal defect. Though in the hour of elemental uproar or peril he was everything that a sailor should be, yet under sudden provocation of strong heart-feeling his voice, otherwise singularly musical, as if expressive of the harmony within, was apt to develop an organic hesitancy, in fact more or less of a stutter or even worse. In this particular Billy was a striking instance that the arch interferer, the envious marplot of Eden,[9] still has more or less to do with every human consignment to this planet of Earth. In every case, one way or another he is sure to slip in his little card, as much as to remind us—I too have a hand here.

The avowal of such an imperfection in the Handsome Sailor should be evidence not alone that he is not presented as a conventional hero, but also that the story in which he is the main figure is no romance.

3

A T THE TIME of Billy Budd's arbitrary enlistment into
the *Bellipotent* that ship was on her way to join the
Mediterranean fleet. No long time elapsed before the
junction was effected. As one of that fleet the seventy-
four participated in its movements, though at times on
account of her superior sailing qualities, in the absence
of frigates, dispatched on separate duty as a scout and at
times on less temporary service. But with all this the
story has little concernment, restricted as it is to the
inner life of one particular ship and the career of an individual sailor.

It was the summer of 1797. In the April of that year
had occurred the commotion at Spithead followed in
May by a second and yet more serious outbreak in the
fleet at the Nore.[1] The latter is known, and without ex-
aggeration in the epithet, as "the Great Mutiny." It was
indeed a demonstration more menacing to England than
the contemporary manifestoes and conquering and proselyting armies of the French Directory. To the British

17

Empire the Nore Mutiny was what a strike in the fire brigade would be to London threatened by general arson. In a crisis when the kingdom might well have anticipated the famous signal that some years later published along the naval line of battle what it was that upon occasion England expected of Englishmen; *that* was the time when at the mastheads of the three-deckers and seventy-fours moored in her own roadstead—a fleet the right arm of a Power then all but the sole free conservative one of the Old World—the bluejackets, to be numbered by thousands, ran up with huzzas the British colors with the union and cross wiped out; by that cancellation transmuting the flag of founded law and freedom defined, into the enemy's red meteor of unbridled and unbounded revolt. Reasonable discontent growing out of practical grievances in the fleet had been ignited into irrational combustion as by live cinders blown across the Channel from France in flames.[2]

The event converted into irony for a time those spirited strains of Dibdin—as a song-writer no mean auxiliary to the English government at that European conjuncture—strains celebrating, among other things, the patriotic devotion of the British tar: "And as for my life, 'tis the King's!"

Such an episode in the Island's grand naval story her naval historians naturally abridge, one of them (William James) candidly acknowledging that fain would he pass it over did not "impartiality forbid fastidiousness." And yet his mention is less a narration than a reference, having to do hardly at all with details. Nor are these readily to be found in the libraries. Like some other events in every age befalling states everywhere, including America, the Great Mutiny was of such character that national pride along with views of policy would fain shade it off into the historical background. Such events cannot be ignored, but there is a considerate way of historically treating them. If a well-constituted individual refrains from blazoning aught amiss or calamitous in his family, a nation in the like circumstance may without reproach be equally discreet.

Though after parleyings between government and the ringleaders, and concessions by the former as to some glaring abuses, the first uprising—that at Spithead—with difficulty was put down, or matters for the time pacified; yet at the Nore the unforeseen renewal of insurrection on a yet larger scale, and emphasized in the conferences that ensued by demands deemed by the authorities not only inadmissible but aggressively insolent, indicated—if the Red Flag[3] did not sufficiently do so—what was the spirit animating the men. Final suppression, however, there was; but only made possible perhaps by the unswerving loyalty of the marine corps and a voluntary resumption of loyalty among influential sections of the crews.

To some extent the Nore Mutiny may be regarded as analogous to the distempering irruption of contagious fever in a frame constitutionally sound, and which anon throws it off.

At all events, of these thousands of mutineers were some of the tars who not so very long afterwards—whether wholly prompted thereto by patriotism, or pugnacious instinct, or by both—helped to win a coronet for Nelson at the Nile, and the naval crown of crowns for him at Trafalgar.[4] To the mutineers, those battles and especially Trafalgar were a plenary absolution and a grand one. For all that goes to make up scenic naval display and heroic magnificence in arms, those battles, especially Trafalgar, stand unmatched in human annals.

4

IN THIS MATTER of writing, resolve as one may to keep to the main road, some bypaths have an enticement not readily to be withstood. I am going to err into such a bypath. If the reader will keep me company I shall be glad. At the least, we can promise ourselves that pleasure which is wickedly said to be in sinning, for a literary sin the divergence will be.

Very likely it is no new remark that the inventions of our time have at last brought about a change in sea warfare in degree corresponding to the revolution in all warfare effected by the original introduction from China into Europe of gunpowder. The first European firearm, a clumsy contrivance, was, as is well known, scouted by no few of the knights as a base implement, good enough peradventure for weavers too craven to stand up crossing steel with steel in frank fight. But as ashore knightly valor, though shorn of its blazonry, did not cease with the knights, neither on the seas—though nowadays in encounters there a certain kind of displayed gallantry be fallen out of date as hardly applicable under changed circumstances—did the nobler qualities of such naval magnates as Don John of Austria, Doria, Van Tromp, Jean Bart, the long line of British admirals, and the American Decaturs of 1812[1] become obsolete with their wooden walls.

Nevertheless, to anybody who can hold the Present at its worth without being inappreciative of the Past, it may be forgiven, if to such an one the solitary old hulk at Portsmouth, Nelson's *Victory*, seems to float there, not alone as the decaying monument of a fame incorruptible, but also as a poetic reproach, softened by its picturesqueness, to the *Monitors*[2] and yet mightier hulls of the European ironclads. And this not altogether because such craft are unsightly, unavoidably lacking the symmetry and grand lines of the old battleships, but equally for other reasons.

There are some, perhaps, who while not altogether inaccessible to that poetic reproach just alluded to, may yet on behalf of the new order be disposed to parry it; and this to the extent of iconoclasm, if need be. For example, prompted by the sight of the star inserted in the *Victory*'s quarter-deck designating the spot where the Great Sailor fell, these martial utilitarians may suggest considerations implying that Nelson's ornate publication of his person in battle was not only unnecessary, but not military, nay, savored of foolhardiness and vanity. They may add, too, that at Trafalgar it was in effect nothing less than a challenge to death; and death came; and that but for his bravado the victorious admiral might possibly have survived the battle, and so, instead of having his sagacious dying injunctions overruled by his immediate successor in command, he himself when the contest was decided might have brought his shattered fleet to anchor, a proceeding which might have averted the deplorable loss of life by shipwreck in the elemental tempest that followed the martial one.

Well, should we set aside the more than disputable point whether for various reasons it was possible to anchor the fleet, then plausibly enough the Benthamites of war[3] may urge the above. But the *might-have-been* is but boggy ground to build on. And, certainly, in foresight as to the larger issue of an encounter, and anxious preparations for it—buoying the deadly way and mapping it out, as at Copenhagen—few commanders have been so painstakingly circumspect as this same reckless declarer of his person in fight.

Personal prudence, even when dictated by quite other than selfish considerations, surely is no special virtue in a military man; while an excessive love of glory, impassioning a less burning impulse, the honest sense of duty, is the first. If the name *Wellington*[4] is not so much of a trumpet to the blood as the simpler name *Nelson,* the reason for this may perhaps be inferred from the above. Alfred[5] in his funeral ode on the victor of Waterloo ventures not to call him the greatest soldier of all time, though in the same ode he invokes Nelson as "the greatest sailor since our world began."

At Trafalgar Nelson on the brink of opening the fight sat down and wrote his last brief will and testament. If under the presentiment of the most magnificent of all victories to be crowned by his own glorious death, a sort of priestly motive led him to dress his person in the jewelled vouchers of his own shining deeds; if thus to have adorned himself for the altar and the sacrifice were indeed vainglory, then affectation and fustian is each more heroic line in the great epics and dramas, since in such lines the poet but embodies in verse those exaltations of sentiment that a nature like Nelson, the opportunity being given, vitalizes into acts.

5

YES, THE OUTBREAK at the Nore was put down. But not every grievance was redressed. If the contractors, for example, were no longer permitted to ply some practices peculiar to their tribe everywhere, such as providing shoddy cloth, rations not sound, or false in the measure; not the less impressment, for one thing, went on. By custom sanctioned for centuries, and judicially maintained by a Lord Chancellor as late as Mansfield,[1] that mode of manning the fleet, a mode now fallen into a sort of abeyance but never formally renounced, it was not practicable to give up in those years. Its abrogation would have crippled the indispensable fleet, one wholly under canvas, no steam power, its innumerable sails and thousands of cannon, everything in short, worked by muscle alone; a fleet the more insatiate in demand for men, because then multiplying its ships of all grades against contingencies present and to come of the convulsed Continent.

Discontent foreran the Two Mutinies, and more or

less it lurkingly survived them. Hence it was not unreasonable to apprehend some return of trouble sporadic or general. One instance of such apprehensions: In the same year with this story, Nelson, then Rear Admiral Sir Horatio, being with the fleet off the Spanish coast, was directed by the admiral in command to shift his pennant[2] from the *Captain* to the *Theseus;* and for this reason: that the latter ship having newly arrived on the station from home, where it had taken part in the Great Mutiny, danger was apprehended from the temper of the men; and it was thought that an officer like Nelson was the one, not indeed to terrorize the crew into base subjection, but to win them, by force of his mere presence and heroic personality, back to an allegiance if not as enthusiastic as his own yet as true.

So it was that for a time, on more than one quarterdeck, anxiety did exist. At sea, precautionary vigilance was strained against relapse. At short notice an engagement might come on. When it did, the lieutenants assigned to batteries felt it incumbent on them, in some instances, to stand with drawn swords behind the men working the guns.

6

B<small>UT ON BOARD</small> the seventy-four in which Billy now swung his hammock, very little in the manner of the men and nothing obvious in the demeanor of the officers would have suggested to an ordinary observer that the Great Mutiny was a recent event. In their general bearing and conduct the commissioned officers of a warship naturally take their tone from the commander, that is if he have that ascendancy of character that ought to be his.

Captain the Honorable Edward Fairfax Vere, to give his full title, was a bachelor of forty or thereabouts, a sailor of distinction even in a time prolific of renowned seamen. Though allied to the higher nobility, his advancement had not been altogether owing to influences connected with that circumstance. He had seen much service, been in various engagements, always acquitting himself as an officer mindful of the welfare of his men, but never tolerating an infraction of discipline; thoroughly versed in the science of his profession, and intrepid to the verge of temerity, though never injudiciously so. For his gallantry in the West Indian waters as flag lieutenant under Rodney in that admiral's crowning victory over De Grasse,[1] he was made a post captain.

Ashore, in the garb of a civilian, scarce anyone would have taken him for a sailor, more especially that he never garnished unprofessional talk with nautical terms, and grave in his bearing, evinced little appreciation of mere humor. It was not out of keeping with these traits that on a passage when nothing demanded his paramount action, he was the most undemonstrative of men. Any landsman observing this gentleman not conspicuous by his stature and wearing no pronounced insignia, emerging from his cabin to the open deck, and noting the silent deference of the officers retiring to leeward, might have taken him for the King's guest, a civilian aboard the King's ship, some highly honorable discreet envoy on his way to an important post. But in fact this unobtrusiveness of demeanor may have proceeded from a certain unaffected modesty of manhood sometimes accompanying a resolute nature, a modesty evinced at all times not calling for pronounced action, which shown in any rank of life suggests a virtue aristocratic in kind. As with some others engaged in various departments of the world's more heroic activities, Captain Vere though practical enough upon occasion would at times betray a certain dreaminess of mood. Standing alone on the weather side of the quarter-deck, one hand holding by the rigging, he would absently gaze off at the blank sea. At the presentation to him then of some minor matter interrupting the current of his thoughts, he would show more or less irascibility; but instantly he would control it.

In the navy he was popularly known by the appellation "Starry Vere." How such a designation happened to fall upon one who whatever his sterling qualities was without any brilliant ones, was in this wise: A favorite kinsman, Lord Denton, a freehearted fellow, had been the first to meet and congratulate him upon his return to England from his West Indian cruise; and but the day previous turning over a copy of Andrew Marvell's[2] poems had lighted, not for the first time, however, upon the lines entitled "Appleton House," the name of one of the seats of their common ancestor, a hero in the German wars of the seventeenth century, in which poem occur the lines:

> This 'tis to have been from the first
> In a domestic heaven nursed,
> Under the discipline severe
> Of Fairfax and the starry Vere.

And so, upon embracing his cousin fresh from Rodney's great victory wherein he had played so gallant a part, brimming over with just family pride in the sailor of their house, he exuberantly exclaimed, "Give ye joy, Ed; give ye joy, my starry Vere!" This got currency, and the novel prefix serving in familiar parlance readily to distinguish the *Bellipotent*'s captain from another Vere his senior, a distant relative, an officer of like rank in the navy, it remained permanently attached to the surname.

7

I N VIEW OF THE PART that the commander of the *Bellipotent* plays in scenes shortly to follow, it may be well to fill out that sketch of him outlined in the previous chapter.

Aside from his qualities as a sea officer Captain Vere was an exceptional character. Unlike no few of England's renowned sailors, long and arduous service with signal devotion to it had not resulted in absorbing and *salting* the entire man. He had a marked leaning toward everything intellectual. He loved books, never going to sea without a newly replenished library, compact but of the best. The isolated leisure, in some cases so wearisome, falling at intervals to commanders even during a war cruise, never was tedious to Captain Vere. With nothing of that literary taste which less heeds the thing conveyed than the vehicle, his bias was toward those books to which every serious mind of superior order occupying any active post of authority in the world naturally inclines: books treating of actual men and events no matter of what era—history, biography, and unconventional writers like Montaigne,[1] who, free from cant and convention, honestly and in the spirit of common sense philosophize upon realities. In this line of reading he found confirmation of his own more reserved thoughts— confirmation which he had vainly sought in social converse, so that as touching most fundamental topics, there had got to be established in him some positive convictions which he forefelt would abide in him essentially unmodified so long as his intelligent part remained unimpaired. In view of the troubled period in which his lot was cast, this was well for him. His settled convictions were as a dike against those invading waters of novel opinion social, political, and otherwise, which carried away as in a torrent no few minds in those days, minds by nature not inferior to his own. While other members of that aristocracy to which by birth he belonged were incensed at the innovators mainly because their theories were inimical to the privileged classes, Captain Vere disinterestedly opposed them not alone because they seemed to him insusceptible of embodiment in lasting institutions, but at war with the peace of the world and the true welfare of mankind.

With minds less stored than his and less earnest, some officers of his rank, with whom at times he would necessarily consort, found him lacking in the companionable quality, a dry and bookish gentleman, as they deemed. Upon any chance withdrawal from their company one would be apt to say to another something like this: "Vere is a noble fellow, Starry Vere. 'Spite the gazettes, Sir Horatio" (meaning him who became Lord Nelson) "is at bottom scarce a better seaman or fighter. But between you and me now, don't you think there is a queer streak of the pedantic running through him? Yes, like the King's yarn in a coil of navy rope?"

Some apparent ground there was for this sort of confidential criticism; since not only did the captain's discourse never fall into the jocosely familiar, but in illustrating of any point touching the stirring personages and events of the time he would be as apt to cite some historic character or incident of antiquity as he would be to cite from the moderns. He seemed unmindful of the circumstance that to his bluff company such remote allusions, however pertinent they might really be, were altogether alien to men whose reading was mainly confined to the journals.[2] But considerateness in such matters is not easy to natures constituted like Captain Vere's. Their honesty prescribes to them directness, sometimes far-reaching like that of a migratory fowl that in its flight never heeds when it crosses a frontier.

8

THE LIEUTENANTS and other commissioned gentle-men forming Captain Vere's staff it is not necessary here to particularize, nor needs it to make any mention of any of the warrant officers. But among the petty officers was one who, having much to do with the story, may as well be forthwith introduced. His portrait I essay, but shall never hit it. This was John Claggart, the master-at-arms. But that sea title may to landsmen seem somewhat equivocal. Originally, doubtless, that petty officer's function was the instruction of the men in the use of arms, sword or cutlass. But very long ago, owing to the advance in gunnery making hand-to-hand encounters less frequent and giving to niter and sulphur the pre-eminence over steel, that function ceased; the master-at-arms of a great warship becoming a sort of chief of police charged among other matters with the duty of preserving order on the populous lower gun decks.

Claggart was a man about five-and-thirty, somewhat spare and tall, yet of no ill figure upon the whole. His hand was too small and shapely to have been accustomed to hard toil. The face was a notable one, the features all except the chin cleanly cut as those on a Greek medallion; yet the chin, beardless as Tecumseh's,[1] had something of strange protuberant broadness in its make that recalled the prints of the Reverend Dr. Titus Oates, the historic deponent with the clerical drawl in the time of Charles II and the fraud of the alleged Popish Plot.[2] It served Claggart in his office that his eye could cast a tutoring glance. His brow was of the sort phrenologically[3] associated with more than average intellect; silken jet curls partly clustering over it, making a foil to the pallor below, a pallor tinged with a faint shade of amber akin to the hue of time-tinted marbles of old. This complexion, singularly contrasting with the red or deeply bronzed visages of the sailors, and in part the result of his official seclusion from the sunlight, though it was not exactly displeasing, nevertheless seemed to hint of something defective or abnormal in the constitution and blood. But his general aspect and manner were so suggestive of an education and career incongruous with his naval function that when not actively engaged in it he looked like a man of high quality, social and moral, who for reasons of his own was keeping incog. Nothing was known of his former life. It might be that he was an Englishman; and yet there lurked a bit of accent in his speech suggesting that possibly he was not such by birth, but through naturalization in early childhood. Among certain grizzled sea gossips of the gun decks and forecastle went a rumor perdue that the master-at-arms was a *chevalier*[4] who had volunteered into the King's navy by way of compounding for some mysterious swindle whereof he had been arraigned at the King's Bench. The fact that nobody could substantiate this report was, of course, nothing against its secret currency. Such a rumor once started on the gun decks in reference to almost anyone below the rank of a commissioned officer would, during the period assigned to this narrative, have seemed not altogether wanting in credibility to the tarry old wiseacres of a man-of-war crew. And indeed a man of Claggart's accomplishments, without prior nautical experience entering the navy at mature life, as he did, and necessarily allotted at the start to the lowest grade in it; a man too who never made allusion to his previous life ashore; these were circumstances which in the dearth of exact knowledge as to his true antecedents opened to the invidious a vague field for unfavorable surmise.

But the sailors' dogwatch gossip concerning him derived a vague plausibility from the fact that now for some period the British navy could so little afford to be squeamish in the matter of keeping up the muster rolls, that not only were press gangs notoriously abroad both afloat and ashore, but there was little or no secret about another matter, namely, that the London police were at liberty to capture any able-bodied suspect, any questionable fellow at large, and summarily ship him to the dockyard or fleet. Furthermore, even among voluntary enlistments there were instances where the motive thereto partook neither of patriotic impulse nor yet of a random desire to experience a bit of sea life and martial adventure. Insolvent debtors of minor grade, together with the promiscuous lame ducks of morality, found in the navy a convenient and secure refuge, secure because, once enlisted aboard a King's ship, they were as much in sanctuary as the transgressor of the Middle Ages harboring himself under the shadow of the altar.

Such sanctioned irregularities, which for obvious reasons the government would hardly think to parade at the time and which consequently, and as affecting the least influential class of mankind, have all but dropped into oblivion, lend color to something for the truth whereof I do not vouch, and hence have some scruple in stating; something I remember having seen in print though the book I cannot recall; but the same thing was personally communicated to me now more than forty years ago by an old pensioner in a cocked hat with whom I had a most interesting talk on the terrace at Greenwich, a Baltimore Negro, a Trafalgar man. It was to this effect: In the case of a warship short of hands whose speedy sailing was imperative, the deficient quota, in lack of any other way of making it good, would be eked out by drafts culled direct from the jails. For reasons previously suggested it would not perhaps be easy at the present day directly to prove or disprove the allegation. But allowed as a verity, how significant would it be of England's straits at the time confronted by those wars which like a flight of harpies rose shrieking from the din and dust of the fallen Bastille.[5] That era appears measurably clear to us who look back at it, and but read of it. But to the grandfathers of us graybeards, the more thoughtful of them, the genius of it presented an aspect like that of Camoëns' Spirit of the Cape, an eclipsing menace mysterious and prodigious. Not America was exempt from apprehension. At the height of Napoleon's unexampled conquests, there were Americans who had fought at Bunker Hill[6] who looked forward to the possibility that the Atlantic might prove no barrier against the ultimate schemes of this French portentous upstart from the revolutionary chaos who seemed in act of fulfilling judgment prefigured in the Apocalypse.[7]

But the less credence was to be given to the gun-deck talk touching Claggart, seeing that no man holding his office in a man-of-war can ever hope to be popular with the crew. Besides, in derogatory comments upon anyone against whom they have a grudge, or for any reason or no reason mislike, sailors are much like landsmen: they are apt to exaggerate or romance it.

About as much was really known to the *Bellipotent's* tars of the master-at-arms' career before entering the service as an astronomer knows about a comet's travels prior to its first observable appearance in the sky. The verdict of the sea quidnuncs has been cited only by way of showing what sort of moral impression the man made upon rude uncultivated natures whose conceptions of human wickedness were necessarily of the narrowest, limited to ideas of vulgar rascality—a thief among the swinging hammocks during a night watch, or the man-brokers and land-sharks of the seaports.

It was no gossip, however, but fact that though, as before hinted, Claggart upon his entrance into the navy was, as a novice, assigned to the least honorable section of a man-of-war's crew, embracing the drudgery, he did not long remain there. The superior capacity he immediately evinced, his constitutional sobriety, an ingratiating deference to superiors, together with a peculiar ferreting genius manifested on a singular occasion; all this, capped by a certain austere patriotism, abruptly advanced him to the position of master-at-arms.

Of this maritime chief of police the ship's corporals, so called, were the immediate subordinates, and compliant ones; and this, as is to be noted in some business departments ashore, almost to a degree inconsistent with entire moral volition. His place put various converging wires of underground influence under the chief's control, capable when astutely worked through his understrappers of operating to the mysterious discomfort, if nothing worse, of any of the sea commonalty.

9

Life in the foretop well agreed with Billy Budd. There, when not actually engaged on the yards yet higher aloft, the topmen, who as such had been picked out for youth and activity, constituted an aerial club lounging at ease against the smaller stun'sails rolled up into cushions, spinning yarns like the lazy gods, and frequently amused with what was going on in the busy world of the decks below. No wonder then that a young fellow of Billy's disposition was well content in such society. Giving no cause of offense to anybody, he was always alert at a call. So in the merchant service it had been with him. But now such a punctiliousness in duty was shown that his topmates would sometimes good-naturedly laugh at him for it. This heightened alacrity had its cause, namely, the impression made upon him by the first formal gangway-punishment he had ever witnessed, which befell the day following his impressment. It had been incurred by a little fellow, young, a novice afterguardsman absent from his assigned post when the ship was being put about; a dereliction resulting in a rather serious hitch to that maneuver, one demanding instantaneous promptitude in letting go and making fast. When Billy saw the culprit's naked back under the scourge, gridironed with red welts and worse, when he marked the dire expression in the liberated man's face as with his woolen shirt flung over him by the executioner he rushed forward from the spot to bury himself in the crowd, Billy was horrified. He resolved that never through remissness would he make himself liable to such a visitation or do or omit aught that might merit even verbal reproof. What then was his surprise and concern when ultimately he found himself getting into petty trouble occasionally about such matters as the stowage of his bag or something amiss in his hammock, matters under the police oversight of the ship's corporals of the lower decks, and which brought down on him a vague threat from one of them.

So heedful in all things as he was, how could this be? He could not understand it, and it more than vexed him. When he spoke to his young topmates about it they were either lightly incredulous or found something comical in his unconcealed anxiety. "Is it your bag, Billy?" said one. "Well, sew yourself up in it, bully boy, and then you'll be sure to know if anybody meddles with it."

Now there was a veteran aboard who because his years began to disqualify him for more active work had been recently assigned duty as mainmastman in his watch, looking to the gear belayed at the rail roundabout that great spar near the deck. At off-times the foretopman had picked up some acquaintance with him, and now in his trouble it occurred to him that he might be the sort of person to go to for wise counsel. He was an old Dansker[1] long anglicized in the service, of few words, many wrinkles, and some honorable scars. His wizened face, time-tinted and weather-stained to the complexion of an antique parchment, was here and there peppered blue by the chance explosion of a gun cartridge in action.

He was an *Agamemnon* man, some two years prior to the time of this story having served under Nelson when still captain in that ship immortal in naval memory, which dismantled and in part broken up to her bare ribs is seen a grand skeleton in Haden's etching.[2] As one of a boarding party from the *Agamemnon* he had received a cut slantwise along one temple and cheek leaving a long pale scar like a streak of dawn's light falling athwart the dark visage. It was on account of that scar and the affair in which it was known that he had received it, as well as from his blue-peppered complexion, that the Dansker went among the *Bellipotent*'s crew by the name of "Board-Her-in-the-Smoke."

Now the first time that his small weasel eyes happened to light on Billy Budd, a certain grim internal merriment set all his ancient wrinkles into antic play. Was it that his eccentric unsentimental old sapience, primitive in its kind, saw or thought it saw something which in contrast with the warship's environment looked oddly incongruous in the Handsome Sailor? But after slyly studying him at intervals, the old Merlin's[3] equivocal merriment was modified; for now when the twain would meet, it would start in his face a quizzing sort of look, but it would be but momentary and sometimes replaced by an expression of speculative query as to what might eventually befall a nature like that, dropped into a world not without some mantraps and against whose subtleties simple courage lacking experience and address, and without any touch of defensive ugliness, is of little avail;

and where such innocence as man is capable of does yet in a moral emergency not always sharpen the faculties or enlighten the will.

However it was, the Dansker in his ascetic way rather took to Billy. Nor was this only because of a certain philosophic interest in such a character. There was another cause. While the old man's eccentricities, sometimes bordering on the ursine, repelled the juniors, Billy, undeterred thereby, revering him as a salt hero, would make advances, never passing the old *Agamemnon* man without a salutation marked by that respect which is seldom lost on the aged, however crabbed at times or whatever their station in life.

There was a vein of dry humor, or what not, in the mastman; and, whether in freak of patriarchal irony touching Billy's youth and athletic frame, or for some other and more recondite reason, from the first in addressing him he always substituted *Baby* for Billy, the Dansker in fact being the originator of the name by which the foretopman eventually became known aboard ship.

Well then, in his mysterious little difficulty going in quest of the wrinkled one, Billy found him off duty in a dogwatch ruminating by himself, seated on a shot box of the upper gun deck, now and then surveying with a somewhat cynical regard certain of the more swaggering promenaders there. Billy recounted his trouble, again wondering how it all happened. The salt seer attentively listened, accompanying the foretopman's recital with queer twitchings of his wrinkles and problematical little sparkles of his small ferret eyes. Making an end of his story, the foretopman asked, "And now, Dansker, do tell me what you think of it."

The old man, shoving up the front of his tarpaulin and deliberately rubbing the long slant scar at the point where it entered the thin hair, laconically said, "Baby Budd, *Jemmy Legs*" (meaning the master-at-arms) "is down on you."

"*Jemmy Legs!*" ejaculated Billy, his welkin eyes expanding. "What for? Why, he calls me 'the sweet and pleasant young fellow,' they tell me."

"Does he so?" grinned the grizzled one; then said, "Ay, Baby lad, a sweet voice has Jemmy Legs."

"No, not always. But to me he has. I seldom pass him but there comes a pleasant word."

"And that's because he's down upon you, Baby Budd."

Such reiteration, along with the manner of it, incomprehensible to a novice, disturbed Billy almost as much as the mystery for which he had sought explanation. Something less unpleasingly oracular he tried to extract; but the old sea Chiron, thinking perhaps that for the nonce he had sufficiently instructed his young Achilles,[4] pursed his lips, gathered all his wrinkles together, and would commit himself to nothing further.

Years, and those experiences which befall certain shrewder men subordinated lifelong to the will of superiors, all this had developed in the Dansker the pithy guarded cynicism that was his leading characteristic.

10

THE NEXT DAY an incident served to confirm Billy Budd in his incredulity as to the Dansker's strange summing up of the case submitted. The ship at noon, going large before the wind, was rolling on her course, and he below at dinner and engaged in some sportful talk with the members of his mess, chanced in a sudden lurch to spill the entire contents of his soup pan upon the new-scrubbed deck. Claggart, the master-at-arms, official rattan[1] in hand, happened to be passing along the battery in a bay of which the mess was lodged, and the greasy liquid streamed just across his path. Stepping over it, he was proceeding on his way without comment, since the matter was nothing to take notice of under the circumstances, when he happened to observe who it was that had done the spilling. His countenance changed. Pausing, he was about to ejaculate something hasty at the sailor, but checked himself, and pointing down to the streaming soup, playfully tapped him from behind with his rattan, saying in a low musical voice peculiar to him at times, "Handsomely done, my lad! And handsome is as handsome did it, too!" And with that passed on. Not noted by Billy as not coming within his view was the involuntary smile, or rather grimace, that accompanied Claggart's equivocal words. Aridly it drew down the thin corners of his shapely mouth. But everybody taking his remark as meant for humorous, and at which therefore as coming from a superior they were bound to laugh "with counterfeited glee," acted accordingly; and Billy, tickled, it may be, by the allusion to his being the Handsome Sailor, merrily joined in; then addressing his messmates exclaimed, "There now, who says that Jemmy Legs is down on me!"

"And who said he was, Beauty?" demanded one Donald with some surprise. Whereat the foretopman looked a little foolish, recalling that it was only one person, Board-Her-in-the-Smoke, who had suggested what to him was the smoky idea that this master-at-arms was in any peculiar way hostile to him. Meantime that functionary, resuming his path, must have momentarily worn some expression less guarded than that of the bitter smile, usurping the face from the heart—some distorting expression perhaps, for a drummer-boy heedlessly frolicking along from the opposite direction and chancing to come into light collision with his person was strangely disconcerted by his aspect. Nor was the impression lessened when the official, impetuously giving him a sharp cut with the rattan, vehemently exclaimed, "Look where you go!"

11

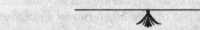

WHAT WAS THE MATTER with the master-at-arms? And, be the matter what it might, how could it have direct relation to Billy Budd, with whom prior to the affair of the spilled soup he had never come into any special contact official or otherwise? What indeed could the trouble have to do with one so little inclined to give offense as the merchant-ship's "peacemaker," even him who in Claggart's own phrase was "the sweet and pleasant young fellow"? Yes, why should Jemmy Legs, to borrow the Dansker's expression, be "down" on the Handsome Sailor? But, at heart and not for nothing, as the late chance encounter may indicate to the discerning, down on him, secretly down on him, he assuredly was.

Now to invent something touching the more private career of Claggart, something involving Billy Budd, of which something the latter should be wholly ignorant, some romantic incident implying that Claggart's knowledge of the young bluejacket began at some period anterior to catching sight of him on board the seventy-four—all this, not so difficult to do, might avail in a way more or less interesting to account for whatever of enigma may appear to lurk in the case. But in fact there was nothing of the sort. And yet the cause necessarily to be assumed as the sole one assignable is in its very realism as much charged with that prime element of Radcliffian romance, the mysterious, as any that the ingenuity of the author of *The Mysteries of Udolpho*[1] could devise. For what can more partake of the mysterious than an antipathy spontaneous and profound such as is evoked in certain exceptional mortals by the mere aspect of some other mortal, however harmless he may be, if not called forth by this very harmlessness itself?

Now there can exist no irritating juxtaposition of dissimilar personalities comparable to that which is possible aboard a great warship fully manned and at sea. There, every day among all ranks, almost every man comes into more or less of contact with almost every other man. Wholly there to avoid even the sight of an aggravating object one must needs give it Jonah's toss or jump overboard himself. Imagine how all this might eventually operate on some peculiar human creature the direct reverse of a saint!

But for the adequate comprehending of Claggart by a normal nature these hints are insufficient. To pass from a normal nature to him one must cross "the deadly space between." And this is best done by indirection.

Long ago an honest scholar,[2] my senior, said to me in reference to one who like himself is now no more, a man so unimpeachably respectable that against him nothing was ever openly said though among the few something was whispered, "Yes, X——— is a nut not to be cracked by the tap of a lady's fan. You are aware that I am the adherent of no organized religion, much less of any philosophy built into a system. Well, for all that, I think that to try and get into X———, enter his labyrinth and get out again, without a clue derived from some source other than what is known as 'knowledge of the world'—that were hardly possible, at least for me."

"Why," said I, "X———, however singular a study to some, is yet human, and knowledge of the world assuredly implies the knowledge of human nature, and in most of its varieties."

"Yes, but a superficial knowledge of it, serving ordinary purposes. But for anything deeper, I am not certain whether to know the world and to know human nature be not two distinct branches of knowledge, which while they may coexist in the same heart, yet either may exist with little or nothing of the other. Nay, in an average man of the world, his constant rubbing with it blunts that finer spiritual insight indispensable to the understanding of the essential in certain exceptional characters, whether evil ones or good. In a matter of some importance I have seen a girl wind an old lawyer about her little finger. Nor was it the dotage of senile love. Nothing of the sort. But he knew law better than he knew the girl's heart. Coke and Blackstone[3] hardly shed so much light into obscure spiritual places as the Hebrew prophets. And who were they? Mostly recluses."

At the time, my inexperience was such that I did not quite see the drift of all this. It may be that I see it now. And, indeed, if that lexicon which is based on Holy Writ were any longer popular, one might with less difficulty define and denominate certain phenomenal men. As it is, one must turn to some authority not liable to the charge of being tinctured with the biblical element.

In a list of definitions included in the authentic translation of Plato, a list attributed to him, occurs this: "Natural Depravity:[4] a depravity according to nature," a definition which, though savoring of Calvinism,[5] by no means involves Calvin's dogma as to total mankind. Evidently its intent makes it applicable but to individuals. Not many are the examples of this depravity which the gallows and jail supply. At any rate, for notable instances, since these have no vulgar alloy of the brute in them, but invariably are dominated by intellectuality, one must go elsewhere. Civilization, especially if of the austerer sort, is auspicious to it. It folds itself in the mantle of respectability. It has its certain negative virtues serving as silent auxiliaries. It never allows wine to get within its guard. It is not going too far to say that it is without vices or small sins. There is a phenomenal pride in it that excludes them. It is never mercenary or avaricious. In short, the depravity here meant partakes nothing of the sordid or sensual. It is serious, but free from acerbity. Though no flatterer of mankind it never speaks ill of it.

But the thing which in eminent instances signalizes so exceptional a nature is this: Though the man's even temper and discreet bearing would seem to intimate a mind peculiarly subject to the law of reason, not the less in heart he would seem to riot in complete exemption from that law, having apparently little to do with reason further than to employ it as an ambidexter implement for effecting the irrational. That is to say: Toward the accomplishment of an aim which in wantonness of atrocity would seem to partake of the insane, he will direct a cool judgment sagacious and sound. These men are madmen, and of the most dangerous sort, for their lunacy is not continuous, but occasional, evoked by some special object; it is protectively secretive, which is as much as to say it is self-contained, so that when, moreover, most active it is to the average mind not distinguishable from sanity, and for the reason above suggested: that whatever its aims may be—and the aim is never declared—the method and the outward proceeding are always perfectly rational.

Now something such an one was Claggart, in whom was the mania of an evil nature, not engendered by vicious training or corrupting books or licentious living, but born with him and innate, in short "a depravity according to nature."

Dark sayings are these, some will say. But why? Is it because they somewhat savor of Holy Writ in its phrase "mystery of iniquity"?[6] If they do, such savor was far enough from being intended, for little will it commend these pages to many a reader of today.

The point of the present story turning on the hidden nature of the master-at-arms has necessitated this chapter. With an added hint or two in connection with the incident at the mess, the resumed narrative must be left to vindicate, as it may, its own credibility.

12

THAT CLAGGART'S FIGURE was not amiss, and his face, save the chin, well molded, has already been said. Of these favorable points he seemed not insensible, for he was not only neat but careful in his dress. But the form of Billy Budd was heroic; and if his face was without the intellectual look of the pallid Claggart's, not the less was it lit, like his, from within, though from a different source. The bonfire in his heart made luminous the rose-tan in his cheek.

In view of the marked contrast between the persons of the twain, it is more than probable that when the master-at-arms in the scene last given applied to the sailor the proverb "Handsome is as handsome does," he there let escape an ironic inkling, not caught by the young sailors who heard it, as to what it was that had first moved him against Billy, namely, his significant personal beauty.

Now envy and antipathy, passions irreconcilable in reason, nevertheless in fact may spring conjoined like

Chang and Eng[1] in one birth. Is Envy then such a monster? Well, though many an arraigned mortal has in hopes of mitigated penalty pleaded guilty to horrible actions, did ever anybody seriously confess to envy? Something there is in it universally felt to be more shameful than even felonious crime. And not only does everybody disown it, but the better sort are inclined to incredulity when it is in earnest imputed to an intelligent man. But since its lodgment is in the heart not the brain, no degree of intellect supplies a guarantee against it. But Claggart's was no vulgar form of the passion. Nor, as directed toward Billy Budd, did it partake of that streak of apprehensive jealousy that marred Saul's visage perturbedly brooding on the comely young David.[2] Claggart's envy struck deeper. If askance he eyed the good looks, cheery health, and frank enjoyment of young life in Billy Budd, it was because these went along with a nature that, as Claggart magnetically felt, had in its simplicity never willed malice or experienced the reactionary bite of that serpent. To him, the spirit lodged within Billy, and looking out from his welkin eyes as from windows, that ineffability it was which made the dimple in his dyed cheek, suppled his joints, and dancing in his yellow curls made him preeminently the Handsome Sailor. One person excepted, the master-at-arms was perhaps the only man in the ship intellectually capable of adequately appreciating the moral phenomenon presented in Billy Budd. And the insight but intensified his passion, which assuming various secret forms within him, at times assumed that of cynic disdain, disdain of innocence—to be nothing more than innocent! Yet in an aesthetic way he saw the charm of it, the courageous free-and-easy temper of it, and fain would have shared it, but he despaired of it.

With no power to annul the elemental evil in him, though readily enough he could hide it; apprehending the good, but powerless to be it; a nature like Claggart's, surcharged with energy as such natures almost invariably are, what recourse is left to it but to recoil upon itself and, like the scorpion for which the Creator alone is responsible, act out to the end the part allotted it.

13

PASSION, AND PASSION in its profoundest, is not a thing demanding a palatial stage whereon to play its part. Down among the groundlings, among the beggars and rakers of the garbage, profound passion is enacted. And the circumstances that provoke it, however trivial or mean, are no measure of its power. In the present instance the stage is a scrubbed gun deck, and one of the external provocations a man-of-war's man's spilled soup.

Now when the master-at-arms noticed whence came that greasy fluid streaming before his feet, he must have taken it—to some extent wilfully, perhaps—not for the mere accident it assuredly was, but for the sly escape of a spontaneous feeling on Billy's part more or less answering to the antipathy on his own. In effect a foolish demonstration, he must have thought, and very harmless, like the futile kick of a heifer, which yet were the heifer a shod stallion would not be so harmless. Even so was it that into the gall of Claggart's envy he infused the vitriol of his contempt. But the incident confirmed to him certain telltale reports purveyed to his ear by "Squeak," one of his more cunning corporals, a grizzled little man, so nicknamed by the sailors on account of his squeaky voice and sharp visage ferreting about the dark corners of the lower decks after interlopers, satirically suggesting to them the idea of a rat in a cellar.

From his chief's employing him as an implicit tool in laying little traps for the worriment of the foretopman—for it was from the master-at-arms that the petty persecutions heretofore adverted to had proceeded—the corporal, having naturally enough concluded that his master could have no love for the sailor, made it his business, faithful understrapper that he was, to foment the ill blood by perverting to his chief certain innocent frolics of the good-natured foretopman, besides inventing for his mouth sundry contumelious epithets he claimed to have overheard him let fall. The master-at-arms never suspected the veracity of these reports, more especially as to the epithets, for he well knew how secretly unpopular may become a master-at-arms, at least a master-at-arms of those days, zealous in his function, and how the bluejackets shoot at him in private their raillery and wit; the nickname by which he goes among them (Jemmy Legs) implying under the form of merriment their cherished disrespect and dislike. But in view of the greediness of hate for pabulum it hardly needed a purveyor to feed Claggart's passion.

An uncommon prudence is habitual with the subtler depravity, for it has everything to hide. And in case of an injury but suspected, its secretiveness voluntarily cuts it off from enlightenment or disillusion; and, not unreluctantly, action is taken upon surmise as upon certainty. And the retaliation is apt to be in monstrous disproportion to the supposed offense; for when in anybody was revenge in its exactions aught else but an inordinate usurer? But how with Claggart's conscience? For though consciences are unlike as foreheads, every intelligence, not excluding the scriptural devils who "believe and tremble," has one. But Claggart's conscience being but the lawyer to his will, made ogres of trifles, probably arguing that the motive imputed to Billy in spilling the soup just when he did, together with the epithets alleged, these, if nothing more, made a strong case against him; nay, justified animosity into a sort of retributive righteousness. The Pharisee is the Guy Fawkes[1] prowling in the hid chambers underlying some natures like Claggart's. And they can really form no conception of an unreciprocated malice. Probably the master-at-arms' clandestine persecution of Billy was started to try the temper of the man; but it had not developed any quality in him that enmity could make official use of or even pervert into plausible self-justification; so that the occurrence at the mess, petty if it were, was a welcome one to that peculiar conscience assigned to be the private mentor of Claggart; and, for the rest, not improbably it put him upon new experiments.

14

Not many days after the last incident narrated, something befell Billy Budd that more graveled him than aught that had previously occurred.

It was a warm night for the latitude; and the foretopman, whose watch at the time was properly below, was dozing on the uppermost deck whither he had ascended from his hot hammock, one of hundreds suspended so closely wedged together over a lower gun deck that there was little or no swing to them. He lay as in the shadow of a hillside, stretched under the lee of the booms, a piled ridge of spare spars amidships between foremast and mainmast among which the ship's largest boat, the launch, was stowed. Alongside of three other slumberers from below, he lay near that end of the booms which approaches the foremast; his station aloft on duty as a foretopman being just over the deck-station of the forecastlemen, entitling him according to usage to make himself more or less at home in that neighborhood.

Presently he was stirred into semiconsciousness by somebody, who must have previously sounded the sleep of the others, touching his shoulder, and then, as the foretopman raised his head, breathing into his ear in a quick whisper, "Slip into the lee forechains, Billy; there is something in the wind. Don't speak. Quick, I will meet you there," and disappearing.

Now Billy, like sundry other essentially good-natured ones, had some of the weaknesses inseparable from essential good nature; and among these was a reluctance, almost an incapacity of plumply saying *no* to an abrupt proposition not obviously absurd on the face of it, nor obviously unfriendly, nor iniquitous. And being of warm blood, he had not the phlegm tacitly to negative any proposition by unresponsive inaction. Like his sense of fear, his apprehension as to aught outside of the honest and natural was seldom very quick. Besides, upon the present occasion, the drowse from his sleep still hung upon him.

However it was, he mechanically rose and, sleepily wondering what could be in the wind, betook himself to the designated place, a narrow platform, one of six, outside of the high bulwarks and screened by the great deadeyes and multiple columned lanyards of the shrouds and backstays; and, in a great warship of that time, of dimensions commensurate to the hull's magnitude; a tarry balcony in short, overhanging the sea, and so secluded that one mariner of the *Bellipotent,* a Nonconformist[1] old tar of a serious turn, made it even in daytime his private oratory.

In this retired nook the stranger soon joined Billy Budd. There was no moon as yet; a haze obscured the starlight. He could not distinctly see the stranger's face.

Yet from something in the outline and carriage, Billy took him, and correctly, for one of the afterguard.

"Hist! Billy," said the man, in the same quick cautionary whisper as before. "You were impressed, weren't you? Well, so was I"; and he paused, as to mark the effect. But Billy, not knowing exactly what to make of this, said nothing. Then the other: "We are not the only impressed ones, Billy. There's a gang of us.—Couldn't you—help—at a pinch?"

"What do you mean?" demanded Billy, here thoroughly shaking off his drowse.

"Hist, hist!" the hurried whisper now growing husky. "See here," and the man held up two small objects faintly twinkling in the night-light; "see, they are yours, Billy, if you'll only—"

But Billy broke in, and in his resentful eagerness to deliver himself his vocal infirmity somewhat intruded. "D—d—damme, I don't know what you are d—d—driving at, or what you mean, but you had better g—g—go where you belong!" For the moment the fellow, as confounded, did not stir; and Billy, springing to his feet, said, "If you d—don't start, I'll t—t—toss you back over the r—rail!" There was no mistaking this, and the mysterious emissary decamped, disappearing in the direction of the mainmast in the shadow of the booms.

"Hallo, what's the matter?" here came growling from a forecastleman awakened from his deck-doze by Billy's raised voice. And as the foretopman reappeared and was recognized by him: "Ah, Beauty, is it you? Well, something must have been the matter, for you st—st—stuttered."

"Oh," rejoined Billy, now mastering the impediment, "I found an afterguardsman in our part of the ship here, and I bid him be off where he belongs."

"And is that all you did about it, Foretopman?" gruffly demanded another, an irascible old fellow of brick-colored visage and hair who was known to his associate forecastlemen as "Red Pepper." "Such sneaks I should like to marry to the gunner's daughter!"—by that expression meaning that he would like to subject them to disciplinary castigation over a gun.

However, Billy's rendering of the matter satisfactorily accounted to these inquirers for the brief commotion, since of all the sections of a ship's company the forecastlemen, veterans for the most part and bigoted in their sea prejudices, are the most jealous in resenting territorial encroachments, especially on the part of any of the afterguard, of whom they have but a sorry opinion—chiefly landsmen, never going aloft except to reef or furl the mainsail, and in no wise competent to handle a marlinspike or turn in a deadeye, say.

15

THIS INCIDENT sorely puzzled Billy Budd. It was an entirely new experience, the first time in his life that he had ever been personally approached in underhand intriguing fashion. Prior to this encounter he had known nothing of the afterguardsman, the two men being stationed wide apart, one forward and aloft during his watch, the other on deck and aft.

What could it mean? And could they really be guineas,[1] those two glittering objects the interloper had held up to his (Billy's) eyes? Where could the fellow get guineas? Why, even spare buttons are not so plentiful at sea. The more he turned the matter over, the more he was nonplussed, and made uneasy and discomfited. In his disgustful recoil from an overture which, though he but ill comprehended, he instinctively knew must involve evil of some sort, Billy Budd was like a young horse fresh from the pasture suddenly inhaling a vile whiff from some chemical factory, and by repeated snortings trying to get it out of his nostrils and lungs. This frame of mind barred all desire of holding further parley with the fellow, even were it but for the purpose of gaining some enlightenment as to his design in approaching him. And yet he was not without natural curiosity to see how such a visitor in the dark would look in broad day.

He espied him the following afternoon in his first dogwatch below, one of the smokers on that forward part of the upper gun deck allotted to the pipe. He recognized him by his general cut and build more than by his round freckled face and glassy eyes of pale blue, veiled with lashes all but white. And yet Billy was a bit uncertain whether indeed it were he—yonder chap about his own age chatting and laughing in freehearted way, leaning against a gun; a genial young fellow enough to look at, and something of a rattlebrain, to all appearance. Rather chubby too for a sailor, even an afterguardsman. In short, the last man in the world, one would think, to be overburdened with thoughts, especially those perilous thoughts that must needs belong to a conspirator in any serious project, or even to the underling of such a conspirator.

Although Billy was not aware of it, the fellow, with a sidelong watchful glance, had perceived Billy first, and then noting that Billy was looking at him, thereupon nodded a familiar sort of friendly recognition as to an old acquaintance, without interrupting the talk he was engaged in with the group of smokers. A day or two afterwards, chancing in the evening promenade on a gun deck to pass Billy, he offered a flying word of goodfellowship, as it were, which by its unexpectedness, and equivocalness under the circumstances, so embarrassed Billy that he knew not how to respond to it, and let it go unnoticed.

Billy was now left more at a loss than before. The ineffectual speculations into which he was led were so disturbingly alien to him that he did his best to smother them. It never entered his mind that here was a matter which, from its extreme questionableness, it was his duty as a loyal bluejacket to report in the proper quarter. And, probably, had such a step been suggested to him, he would have been deterred from taking it by the thought, one of novice magnanimity, that it would savor overmuch of the dirty work of a telltale. He kept the thing to himself. Yet upon one occasion he could not forbear a little disburdening himself to the old Dansker, tempted thereto perhaps by the influence of a balmy night when the ship lay becalmed; the twain, silent for the most part, sitting together on deck, their heads propped against the bulwarks. But it was only a partial and anonymous account that Billy gave, the unfounded scruples above referred to preventing full disclosure to anybody. Upon hearing Billy's version, the sage Dansker seemed to divine more than he was told; and after a little meditation, during which his wrinkles were pursed as into a point, quite effacing for the time that quizzing expression his face sometimes wore: "Didn't I say so, Baby Budd?"

"Say what?" demanded Billy.

"Why, *Jemmy Legs* is *down* on you."

"And what," rejoined Billy in amazement, "has *Jemmy Legs* to do with that cracked afterguardsman?"

"Ho, it was an afterguardsman, then. A cat's-paw, a cat's-paw!" And with that exclamation, whether it had reference to a light puff of air just then coming over the calm sea, or a subtler relation to the afterguardsman, there is no telling, the old Merlin gave a twisting wrench with his black teeth at his plug of tobacco, vouchsafing no reply to Billy's impetuous question, though now repeated, for it was his wont to relapse into grim silence when interrogated in skeptical sort as to any of his sententious oracles, not always very clear ones, rather partaking of that obscurity which invests most Delphic[2] deliverances from any quarter.

Long experience had very likely brought this old man to that bitter prudence which never interferes in aught and never gives advice.

16

YES, DESPITE the Dansker's pithy insistence as to the master-at-arms being at the bottom of these strange experiences of Billy on board the *Bellipotent*, the young sailor was ready to ascribe them to almost anybody but the man who, to use Billy's own expression, "always had a pleasant word for him." This is to be wondered at. Yet not so much to be wondered at. In certain matters, some sailors even in mature life remain unsophisticated enough. But a young seafarer of the disposition of our athletic foretopman is much of a child-man. And yet a child's utter innocence is but its blank ignorance, and the innocence more or less wanes as intelligence waxes. But in Billy Budd intelligence, such as it was, had advanced while yet his simplemindedness remained for the most part unaffected. Experience is a teacher indeed; yet did Billy's years make his experience small. Besides, he had none of that intuitive knowledge of the bad which in natures not good or incompletely so foreruns experience, and therefore may pertain, as in some instances it too clearly does pertain, even to youth.

And what could Billy know of man except of man as a mere sailor? And the old-fashioned sailor, the veritable man before the mast, the sailor from boyhood up, he, though indeed of the same species as a landsman, is in some respects singularly distinct from him. The sailor is frankness, the landsman is finesse. Life is not a game with the sailor, demanding the long head—no intricate game of chess where few moves are made in straightforwardness and ends are attained by indirection, an oblique, tedious, barren game hardly worth that poor candle burnt out in playing it.

Yes, as a class, sailors are in character a juvenile race. Even their deviations are marked by juvenility, this more especially holding true with the sailors of Billy's time. Then too, certain things which apply to all sailors do more pointedly operate here and there upon the junior one. Every sailor, too, is accustomed to obey orders without debating them; his life afloat is externally ruled for him; he is not brought into that promiscuous commerce with mankind where unobstructed free agency on equal terms—equal superficially, at least—soon teaches one that unless upon occasion he exercise a distrust keen in proportion to the fairness of the appearance, some foul turn may be served him. A ruled undemonstrative distrustfulness is so habitual, not with businessmen so much as with men who know their kind in less shallow relations than business, namely, certain men of the world, that they come at last to employ it all but unconsciously; and some of them would very likely feel real surprise at being charged with it as one of their general characteristics.

17

BUT AFTER THE LITTLE MATTER at the mess Billy Budd no more found himself in strange trouble at times about his hammock or his clothes bag or what not. As to that smile that occasionally sunned him, and the pleasant passing word, these were, if not more frequent, yet if anything more pronounced than before.

But for all that, there were certain other demonstrations now. When Claggart's unobserved glance happened to light on belted Billy rolling along the upper gun deck in the leisure of the second dogwatch, exchanging passing broadsides of fun with other young promenaders in the crowd, that glance would follow the cheerful sea Hyperion[1] with a settled meditative and melancholy expression, his eyes strangely suffused with incipient feverish tears. Then would Claggart look like the man of sorrows.[2] Yes, and sometimes the melancholy expression would have in it a touch of soft yearning, as if Claggart could even have loved Billy but for fate and ban. But this was an evanescence, and quickly repented of, as it were, by an immitigable look, pinching and shriveling the visage into the momentary semblance of a wrinkled walnut. But sometimes catching sight in advance of the foretopman coming in his direction, he would, upon their nearing, step aside a little to let him pass, dwelling upon Billy for the moment with the glittering dental satire of a Guise.[3] But upon any abrupt unforeseen encounter a red light would flash forth from his eye like a spark from an anvil in a dusk smithy. That quick, fierce light was a strange one, darted from orbs which in repose were of a color nearest approaching a deeper violet, the softest of shades.

Though some of these caprices of the pit could not but be observed by their object, yet were they beyond the construing of such a nature. And the thews of Billy were hardly compatible with that sort of sensitive spiritual organization which in some cases instinctively conveys to ignorant innocence an admonition of the proximity of the malign. He thought the master-at-arms acted in a manner rather queer at times. That was all. But the occasional frank air and pleasant word went for what they purported to be, the young sailor never having heard as yet of the "too fair-spoken man."

Had the foretopman been conscious of having done or said anything to provoke the ill will of the official, it would have been different with him, and his sight might have been purged if not sharpened. As it was, innocence was his blinder.

So was it with him in yet another matter. Two minor officers, the armorer and captain of the hold, with whom he had never exchanged a word, his position in the ship not bringing him into contact with them, these men now for the first began to cast upon Billy, when they chanced to encounter him, that peculiar glance which evidences that the man from whom it comes has been some way tampered with, and to the prejudice of him upon whom the glance lights. Never did it occur to Billy as a thing to be noted or a thing suspicious, though he well knew the fact, that the armorer and captain of the hold, with the ship's yeoman, apothecary, and others of that grade, were by naval usage messmates of the master-at-arms, men with ears convenient to his confidential tongue.

But the general popularity that came from our Handsome Sailor's manly forwardness upon occasion and irresistible good nature, indicating no mental superiority tending to excite an invidious feeling, this good will on the part of most of his shipmates made him the less to concern himself about such mute aspects toward him as those whereto allusion has just been made, aspects he could not so fathom as to infer their whole import.

As to the afterguardsman, though Billy for reasons already given necessarily saw little of him, yet when the two did happen to meet, invariably came the fellow's offhand cheerful recognition, sometimes accompanied by a passing pleasant word or two. Whatever that equivocal young person's original design may really have been, or the design of which he might have been the deputy, certain it was from his manner upon these occasions that he had wholly dropped it.

It was as if his precocity of crookedness (and every vulgar villain is precocious) had for once deceived him, and the man he had sought to entrap as a simpleton had through his very simplicity ignominiously baffled him.

But shrewd ones may opine that it was hardly possible for Billy to refrain from going up to the afterguardsman and bluntly demanding to know his purpose in the initial interview so abruptly closed in the forechains. Shrewd ones may also think it but natural in Billy to set about sounding some of the other impressed men of the ship in order to discover what basis, if any, there was for the emissary's obscure suggestions as to plotting disaffection aboard. Yes, shrewd ones may so think. But something more, or rather something else than mere shrewdness is perhaps needful for the due understanding of such a character as Billy Budd's.

As to Claggart, the monomania[4] in the man—if that indeed it were—as involuntarily disclosed by starts in the manifestations detailed, yet in general covered over by his self-contained and rational demeanor; this, like a subterranean fire, was eating its way deeper and deeper in him. Something decisive must come of it.

18

AFTER THE MYSTERIOUS INTERVIEW in the forechains, the one so abruptly ended there by Billy, nothing especially germane to the story occurred until the events now about to be narrated.

Elsewhere it has been said that in the lack of frigates (of course better sailers than line-of-battle ships) in the English squadron up the Straits at that period, the *Bellipotent 74* was occasionally employed not only as an available substitute for a scout, but at times on detached service of more important kind. This was not alone because of her sailing qualities, not common in a ship of her rate, but quite as much, probably, that the character of her commander, it was thought, specially adapted him for any duty where under unforeseen difficulties a prompt initiative might have to be taken in some matter demanding knowledge and ability in addition to those qualities implied in good seamanship. It was on an expedition of the latter sort, a somewhat distant one, and when the *Bellipotent* was almost at her furthest remove from the fleet, that in the latter part of an afternoon watch she unexpectedly came in sight of a ship of the enemy. It proved to be a frigate. The latter, perceiving through the glass that the weight of men and metal would be heavily against her, invoking her light heels crowded sail to get away. After a chase urged almost against hope and lasting until about the middle of the first dogwatch, she signally succeeded in effecting her escape.

Not long after the pursuit had been given up, and ere the excitement incident thereto had altogether waned away, the master-at-arms, ascending from his cavernous sphere, made his appearance cap in hand by the mainmast respectfully waiting the notice of Captain Vere, then solitary walking the weather side of the quarterdeck, doubtless somewhat chafed at the failure of the pursuit. The spot where Claggart stood was the place allotted to men of lesser grades seeking some more particular interview either with the officer of the deck or the captain himself. But from the latter it was not often that a sailor or petty officer of those days would seek a hearing; only some exceptional cause would, according to established custom, have warranted that.

Presently, just as the commander, absorbed in his reflections, was on the point of turning aft in his promenade, he became sensible of Claggart's presence, and saw the doffed cap held in deferential expectancy. Here be it said that Captain Vere's personal knowledge of this petty officer had only begun at the time of the ship's last sailing from home, Claggart then for the first, in transfer from a ship detained for repairs, supplying on board the *Bellipotent* the place of a previous master-at-arms disabled and ashore.

No sooner did the commander observe who it was that now deferentially stood awaiting his notice than a peculiar expression came over him. It was not unlike that which uncontrollably will flit across the countenance of one at unawares encountering a person who, though known to him indeed, has hardly been long enough known for thorough knowledge, but something in whose aspect nevertheless now for the first provokes a vaguely repellent distaste. But coming to a stand and resuming much of his wonted official manner, save that a sort of impatience lurked in the intonation of the opening word, he said, "Well? What is it, Master-at-arms?"

With the air of a subordinate grieved at the necessity of being a messenger of ill tidings, and while conscientiously determined to be frank yet equally resolved upon shunning overstatement, Claggart at this invitation, or rather summons to disburden, spoke up. What he said, conveyed in the language of no uneducated man, was to the effect following, if not altogether in these words, namely, that during the chase and preparations for the possible encounter he had seen enough to convince him that at least one sailor aboard was a dangerous character in a ship mustering some who not only had taken a guilty part in the late serious troubles, but others also who, like the man in question, had entered His Majesty's service under another form than enlistment.

At this point Captain Vere with some impatience interrupted him: "Be direct, man; say *impressed men*."

Claggart made a gesture of subservience, and proceeded. Quite lately he (Claggart) had begun to suspect that on the gun decks some sort of movement prompted by the sailor in question was covertly going on, but he had not thought himself warranted in reporting the sus-

picion so long as it remained indistinct. But from what
he had that afternoon observed in the man referred to,
the suspicion of something clandestine going on had advanced to a point less removed from certainty. He deeply
felt, he added, the serious responsibility assumed in
making a report involving such possible consequences to
the individual mainly concerned, besides tending to augment those natural anxieties which every naval commander must feel in view of extraordinary outbreaks so
recent as those which, he sorrowfully said it, it needed
not to name.

Now at the first broaching of the matter Captain Vere,
taken by surprise, could not wholly dissemble his disquietude. But as Claggart went on, the former's aspect
changed into restiveness under something in the testifier's manner in giving his testimony. However, he refrained from interrupting him. And Claggart, continuing,
concluded with this: "God forbid, your honor, that the
Bellipotent's should be the experience of the—"

"Never mind that!" here peremptorily broke in the
superior, his face altering with anger, instinctively divining the ship that the other was about to name, one in
which the Nore Mutiny had assumed a singularly trag-
ical character that for a time jeopardized the life of its
commander. Under the circumstances he was indignant
at the purposed allusion. When the commissioned officers themselves were on all occasions very heedful how
they referred to the recent events in the fleet, for a
petty officer unnecessarily to allude to them in the
presence of his captain, this struck him as a most im-
modest presumption. Besides, to his quick sense of
self-respect it even looked under the circumstances
something like an attempt to alarm him. Nor at first

was he without some surprise that one who so far as he had hitherto come under his notice had shown considerable tact in his function should in this particular evince such lack of it.

But these thoughts and kindred dubious ones flitting across his mind were suddenly replaced by an intuitional surmise which, though as yet obscure in form, served practically to affect his reception of the ill tidings. Certain it is that, long versed in everything pertaining to the complicated gun-deck life, which like every other form of life has its secret mines and dubious side, the side popularly disclaimed, Captain Vere did not permit himself to be unduly disturbed by the general tenor of his subordinate's report.

Furthermore, if in view of recent events prompt action should be taken at the first palpable sign of recurring insubordination, for all that, not judicious would it be, he thought, to keep the idea of lingering disaffection alive by undue forwardness in crediting an informer, even if his own subordinate and charged among other things with police surveillance of the crew. This feeling would not perhaps have so prevailed with him were it not that upon a prior occasion the patriotic zeal officially evinced by Claggart had somewhat irritated him as appearing rather supersensible and strained. Furthermore, something even in the official's self-possessed and somewhat ostentatious manner in making his specifications strangely reminded him of a bandsman, a perjurous witness in a capital case before a court-martial ashore of which when a lieutenant he (Captain Vere) had been a member.

Now the peremptory check given to Claggart in the matter of the arrested allusion was quickly followed up by this: "You say that there is at least one dangerous man aboard. Name him."

"William Budd, a foretopman, your honor."

"William Budd!" repeated Captain Vere with unfeigned astonishment. "And mean you the man that Lieutenant Ratcliffe took from the merchantman not very long ago, the young fellow who seems to be so popular with the men—Billy, the Handsome Sailor, as they call him?"

"The same, your honor; but for all his youth and good looks, a deep one. Not for nothing does he insinuate himself into the good will of his shipmates, since at the least they will at a pinch say—all hands will—a good word for him, and at all hazards. Did Lieutenant Ratcliffe happen to tell your honor of that adroit fling of Budd's, jumping up in the cutter's bow under the merchantman's stern when he was being taken off? It is even masked by that sort of good-humored air that at heart he resents his impressment. You have but noted his fair cheek. A mantrap may be under the ruddy-tipped daisies."

Now the Handsome Sailor as a signal figure among the crew had naturally enough attracted the captain's attention from the first. Though in general not very demonstrative to his officers, he had congratulated Lieutenant Ratcliffe upon his good fortune in lighting on such a fine specimen of the *genus homo*,[1] who in the nude might have posed for a statue of young Adam before the Fall. As to Billy's adieu to the ship *Rights-of-Man,* which the boarding lieutenant had indeed reported to him, but, in a deferential way, more as a good story than aught else, Captain Vere, though mistakenly understanding it as a satiric sally, had but thought so much the better of the impressed man for it; as a military sailor, admiring the spirit that could take an arbitrary enlistment so merrily and sensibly. The foretopman's conduct, too, so far as it had fallen under the captain's notice, had confirmed the first happy augury, while the new recruit's qualities as a "sailor-man" seemed to be such that he had thought of recommending him to the executive officer for promotion to a place that would more frequently bring him under his own observation, namely, the captaincy of the mizzentop, replacing there in the starboard watch a man not so young whom partly for that reason he deemed less fitted for the post. Be it parenthesized here that since the mizzentopmen have not to handle such breadths of heavy canvas as the lower sails on the mainmast and foremast, a young man if of the right stuff not only seems best adapted to duty there, but in fact is generally selected for the captaincy of that top, and the company under him are light hands and often but striplings. In sum, Captain Vere had from the beginning deemed Billy Budd to be what in the naval parlance of the time was called a "King's bargain": that is to say, for His Britannic Majesty's navy a capital investment at small outlay or none at all.

After a brief pause, during which the reminiscences above mentioned passed vividly through his mind and he weighed the import of Claggart's last suggestion conveyed in the phrase "mantrap under the daisies," and the more he weighed it the less reliance he felt in the informer's good faith, suddenly he turned upon him and in a low voice demanded: "Do you come to me, Master-at-arms, with so foggy a tale? As to Budd, cite me an act or spoken word of his confirmatory of what you in general charge against him. Stay," drawing nearer to him; "heed what you speak. Just now, and in a case like this, there is a yardarm-end[2] for the false witness."

"Ah, your honor!" sighed Claggart, mildly shaking his shapely head as in sad deprecation of such unmerited severity of tone. Then, bridling—erecting himself as in virtuous self-assertion—he circumstantially alleged certain words and acts which collectively, if credited, led to presumptions mortally inculpating Budd. And for some of these averments, he added, substantiating proof was not far.

With gray eyes impatient and distrustful essaying to fathom to the bottom Claggart's calm violet ones, Captain Vere again heard him out; then for the moment stood ruminating. The mood he evinced, Claggart—himself for the time liberated from the other's scrutiny—steadily regarded with a look difficult to render: a look curious of the operation of his tactics, a look such as might have been that of the spokesman of the envious children of Jacob deceptively imposing upon the troubled patriarch the blood-dyed coat of young Joseph.[3]

Though something exceptional in the moral quality of Captain Vere made him, in earnest encounter with a fellow man, a veritable touchstone of that man's essential nature, yet now as to Claggart and what was really going on in him his feeling partook less of intuitional conviction than of strong suspicion clogged by strange dubieties. The perplexity he evinced proceeded less from aught touching the man informed against—as Claggart doubtless opined—than from considerations how best to act in regard to the informer. At first, indeed, he was naturally for summoning that substantiation of his allegations which Claggart said was at hand. But such a proceeding would result in the matter at once getting abroad, which in the present stage of it, he thought, might undesirably affect the ship's company. If Claggart was a false witness— that closed the affair. And therefore, before trying the accusation, he would first practically test the accuser; and he thought this could be done in a quiet, undemonstrative way.

The measure he determined upon involved a shifting of the scene, a transfer to a place less exposed to observation than the broad quarter-deck. For although the few gunroom officers there at the time had, in due observance of naval etiquette, withdrawn to leeward the moment Captain Vere had begun his promenade on the deck's weather side; and though during the colloquy with Claggart they of course ventured not to diminish the distance; and though throughout the interview Captain Vere's voice was far from high, and Claggart's silvery and low; and the wind in the cordage and the wash of the sea helped the more to put them beyond earshot; nevertheless, the interview's continuance already had attracted observation from some topmen aloft and other sailors in the waist or further forward.

Having determined upon his measures, Captain Vere forthwith took action. Abruptly turning to Claggart, he asked, "Master-at-arms, is it now Budd's watch aloft?"

"No, your honor."

Whereupon, "Mr. Wilkes!" summoning the nearest midshipman. "Tell Albert to come to me." Albert was the captain's hammock-boy, a sort of sea valet in whose discretion and fidelity his master had much confidence. The lad appeared.

"You know Budd, the foretopman?"

"I do, sir."

"Go find him. It is his watch off. Manage to tell him

out of earshot that he is wanted aft. <u>Contrive it that he speaks to nobody.</u> Keep him in talk yourself. And not till you get well aft here, not till then let him know that the place where he is wanted is my cabin. You understand. Go.—Master-at-arms, show yourself on the decks below, and when you think it time for Albert to be coming with his man, stand by quietly to follow the sailor in."

19

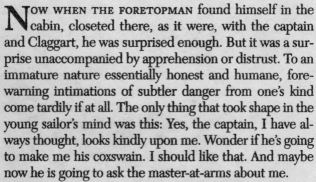

NOW WHEN THE FORETOPMAN found himself in the cabin, closeted there, as it were, with the captain and Claggart, he was surprised enough. But it was a surprise unaccompanied by apprehension or distrust. To an immature nature essentially honest and humane, forewarning intimations of subtler danger from one's kind come tardily if at all. The only thing that took shape in the young sailor's mind was this: Yes, the captain, I have always thought, looks kindly upon me. Wonder if he's going to make me his coxswain. I should like that. And maybe now he is going to ask the master-at-arms about me.

"Shut the door there, sentry," said the commander, "stand without, and let nobody come in.—Now, Master-at-arms, tell this man to his face what you told of him to me," and stood prepared to scrutinize the mutually confronting visages.

With the measured step and calm collected air of an asylum physician approaching in the public hall some patient beginning to show indications of a coming paroxysm, Claggart deliberately advanced within short range of Billy and, mesmerically looking him in the eye, briefly recapitulated the accusation.

Not at first did Billy take it in. When he did, the rose-tan of his cheek looked struck as by white leprosy. He stood like one impaled and gagged. Meanwhile the accuser's eyes, removing not as yet from the blue dilated ones, underwent a phenomenal change, their wonted rich violet color blurring into a muddy purple. Those lights of human intelligence, losing human expression, were gelidly protruding like the alien eyes of certain un-catalogued creatures of the deep. The first mesmeristic glance was one of serpent fascination; the last was as the paralyzing lurch of the torpedo fish.

"Speak, man!" said Captain Vere to the transfixed one, struck by his aspect even more than by Claggart's. "Speak! Defend yourself!" Which appeal caused but a strange dumb gesturing and gurgling in Billy; amaze-ment at such an accusation so suddenly sprung on inex-perienced nonage; this, and, it may be, horror of the accuser's eyes, serving to bring out his lurking defect and in this instance for the time intensifying it into a con-vulsed tongue-tie; while the intent head and entire form straining forward in an agony of ineffectual eagerness to obey the injunction to speak and defend himself, gave an expression to the face like that of a condemned vestal priestess in the moment of being buried alive, and in the first struggle against suffocation.[1]

Though at the time Captain Vere was quite ignorant of Billy's liability to vocal impediment, he now immedi-ately divined it, since vividly Billy's aspect recalled to him that of a bright young schoolmate of his whom he had once seen struck by much the same startling impotence in the act of eagerly rising in the class to be foremost in response to a testing question put to it by the master. Going close up to the young sailor, and laying a soothing hand on his shoulder, he said, "There is no hurry, my boy. Take your time, take your time." Contrary to the effect intended, these words so fatherly in tone, doubtless touching Billy's heart to the quick, prompted yet more violent efforts at utterance—efforts soon ending for the time in confirming the paralysis, and bringing to his face an expression which was as a crucifixion to behold. The next instant, quick as the flame from a discharged cannon at night, his right arm shot out, and Claggart dropped to the deck. Whether intentionally or but owing to the young athlete's superior height, the blow had taken effect full upon the forehead, so shapely and intellectual-looking a feature in the master-at-arms; so that the body fell over lengthwise, like a heavy plank tilted from erectness. A gasp or two, and he lay motionless.

"Fated boy," breathed Captain Vere in tone so low as to be almost a whisper, "what have you done! But here, help me."

The twain raised the felled one from the loins up into a sitting position. The spare form flexibly acquiesced, but inertly. It was like handling a dead snake. They lowered it back. Regaining erectness, Captain Vere with one hand covering his face stood to all appearance as impassive as the object at his feet. Was he absorbed in taking in all the bearings of the event and what was best not only now at once to be done, but also in the sequel? Slowly he uncovered his face; and the effect was as if the moon emerging from eclipse should reappear with quite another aspect than that which had gone into hiding. The father in him, manifested towards Billy thus far in the scene, was replaced by the military disciplinarian. In his official tone he bade the foretopman retire to a stateroom aft (pointing it out), and there remain till thence summoned. This order Billy in silence mechanically obeyed. Then going to the cabin door where it opened on the quarter-deck, Captain Vere said to the sentry without, "Tell somebody to send Albert here." When the lad appeared, his master so contrived it that he should not catch sight of the prone one. "Albert," he said to him, "tell the surgeon I wish to see him. You need not come back till called."

When the surgeon entered—a self-poised character of that grave sense and experience that hardly anything could take him aback—Captain Vere advanced to meet him, thus unconsciously intercepting his view of Claggart, and, interrupting the other's wonted ceremonious salutation, said, "Nay. Tell me how it is with yonder man," directing his attention to the prostrate one.

The surgeon looked, and for all his self-command somewhat started at the abrupt revelation. On Claggart's always pallid complexion, thick black blood was now oozing from nostril and ear. To the gazer's professional eye it was unmistakably no living man that he saw.

"Is it so, then?" said Captain Vere, intently watching him. "I thought it. But verify it." Whereupon the customary tests confirmed the surgeon's first glance, who now, looking up in unfeigned concern, cast a look of intense inquisitiveness upon his superior. But Captain Vere, with one hand to his brow, was standing motionless. Suddenly, catching the surgeon's arm convulsively, he exclaimed, pointing down to the body, "It is the divine judgment on Ananias![2] Look!"

Disturbed by the excited manner he had never before observed in the *Bellipotent*'s captain, and as yet wholly ignorant of the affair, the prudent surgeon nevertheless held his peace, only again looking an earnest interrogatory as to what it was that had resulted in such a tragedy.

But Captain Vere was now again motionless, standing absorbed in thought. Again starting, he vehemently exclaimed, "Struck dead by an angel of God! Yet the angel must hang!"

At these passionate interjections, mere incoherences to the listener as yet unapprised of the antecedents, the surgeon was profoundly discomposed. But now, as recollecting himself, Captain Vere in less passionate tone briefly related the circumstances leading up to the event. "But come; we must dispatch," he added. "Help me to remove him" (meaning the body) "to yonder compartment," designating one opposite that where the foretopman remained immured. Anew disturbed by a request that, as implying a desire for secrecy, seemed unaccountably strange to him, there was nothing for the subordinate to do but comply.

"Go now," said Captain Vere with something of his wonted manner. "Go now. I presently shall call a drumhead court.[3] Tell the lieutenants what has happened, and tell Mr. Mordant" (meaning the captain of marines), "and charge them to keep the matter to themselves."

20

FULL OF DISQUIETUDE and misgiving, the surgeon left the cabin. Was Captain Vere suddenly affected in his mind, or was it but a transient excitement, brought about by so strange and extraordinary a tragedy? As to the drumhead court, it struck the surgeon as impolitic, if nothing more. The thing to do, he thought, was to place Billy Budd in confinement, and in a way dictated by usage, and postpone further action in so extraordinary a case to such time as they should rejoin the squadron, and then refer it to the admiral. He recalled the unwonted agitation of Captain Vere and his excited exclamations, so at variance with his normal manner. Was he unhinged?

But assuming that he is, it is not so susceptible of proof. What then can the surgeon do? No more trying situation is conceivable than that of an officer subordinate under a captain whom he suspects to be not mad, indeed, but yet not quite unaffected in his intellects. To argue his order to him would be insolence. To resist him would be mutiny.

In obedience to Captain Vere, he communicated what had happened to the lieutenants and captain of marines, saying nothing as to the captain's state. They fully shared his own surprise and concern. Like him too, they seemed to think that such a matter should be referred to the admiral.

21

WHO IN THE RAINBOW can draw the line where the violet tint ends and the orange tint begins? Distinctly we see the difference of the colors, but where exactly does the one first blendingly enter into the other? So with sanity and insanity. In pronounced cases there is no question about them. But in some supposed cases, in various degrees supposedly less pronounced, to draw the exact line of demarcation few will undertake, though for a fee becoming considerate some professional experts will. There is nothing namable but that some men will, or undertake to, do it for pay.

Whether Captain Vere, as the surgeon professionally and privately surmised, was really the sudden victim of any degree of aberration, every one must determine for himself by such light as this narrative may afford.

That the unhappy event which has been narrated could not have happened at a worse juncture was but too true. For it was close on the heel of the suppressed insurrections, an aftertime very critical to naval authority, demanding from every English sea commander two qualities not readily interfusable—prudence and rigor. Moreover, there was something crucial in the case.

In the jugglery of circumstances preceding and attending the event on board the *Bellipotent,* and in the light of that martial code whereby it was formally to be judged, innocence and guilt personified in Claggart and Budd in effect changed places. In a legal view the apparent victim of the tragedy was he who had sought to victimize a man blameless; and the indisputable deed of the latter, navally regarded, constituted the most heinous of military crimes. Yet more. The essential right and wrong involved in the matter, the clearer that might be, so much the worse for the responsibility of a loyal sea commander, inasmuch as he was not authorized to determine the matter on that primitive basis.

Small wonder then that the *Bellipotent*'s captain, though in general a man of rapid decision, felt that circumspectness not less than promptitude was necessary. Until he could decide upon his course, and in each detail; and not only so, but until the concluding measure was upon the point of being enacted, he deemed it advisable, in view of all the circumstances, to guard as much as possible against publicity. Here he may or may not have erred. Certain it is, however, that subsequently in the confidential talk of more than one or two gun rooms and cabins he was not a little criticized by some officers, a fact imputed by his friends and vehemently by his cousin Jack Denton to professional jealousy of Starry Vere. Some imaginative ground for invidious comment there was. The maintenance of secrecy in the matter, the confining all knowledge of it for a time to the place where the homicide occurred, the quarter-deck cabin; in these particulars lurked some resemblance to the policy adopted in those tragedies of the palace which have occurred more than once in the capital founded by Peter the Barbarian.[1]

The case indeed was such that fain would the *Bellipotent*'s captain have deferred taking any action whatever respecting it further than to keep the foretopman a close prisoner till the ship rejoined the squadron and then submitting the matter to the judgment of his admiral.

But a true military officer is in one particular like a true monk. Not with more of self-abnegation will the latter keep his vows of monastic obedience than the former his vows of allegiance to martial duty.

Feeling that unless quick action was taken on it, the deed of the foretopman, so soon as it should be known on the gun decks, would tend to awaken any slumbering embers of the Nore among the crew, a sense of the urgency of the case overruled in Captain Vere every other consideration. But though a conscientious disciplinarian, he was no lover of authority for mere authority's sake. Very far was he from embracing opportunities for monopolizing to himself the perils of moral responsibility, none at least that could properly be referred to an official superior or shared with him by his official equals or even subordinates. So thinking, he was glad it would not be at variance with usage to turn the matter over to a summary court of his own officers, reserving to himself, as the one on whom the ultimate accountability would rest, the right of maintaining a supervision of it, or formally or informally interposing at need. Accordingly a drumhead court was summarily convened, he electing the individuals composing it: the first lieutenant, the captain of marines, and the sailing master.

In associating an officer of marines with the sea lieutenant and the sailing master in a case having to do with a sailor, the commander perhaps deviated from general custom. He was prompted thereto by the circumstance that he took that soldier to be a judicious person, thoughtful, and not altogether incapable of grappling with a difficult case unprecedented in his prior experience. Yet even as to him he was not without some latent misgiving, for withal he was an extremely good-natured man, an enjoyer of his dinner, a sound sleeper, and inclined to obesity—a man who though he would always maintain his manhood in battle might not prove altogether reliable in a moral dilemma involving aught of the tragic. As to the first lieutenant and the sailing master, Captain Vere could not but be aware that though honest natures, of approved gallantry upon occasion, their intelligence was mostly confined to the matter of active seamanship and the fighting demands of their profession.

The court was held in the same cabin where the unfortunate affair had taken place. This cabin, the commander's, embraced the entire area under the poop deck. Aft, and on either side, was a small stateroom, the one now temporarily a jail and the other a dead-house, and a yet smaller compartment, leaving a space between expanding forward into a goodly oblong of length coinciding with the ship's beam. A skylight of moderate dimension was overhead, and at each end of the oblong space were two sashed porthole windows easily convertible back into embrasures for short carronades.

All being quickly in readiness, Billy Budd was arraigned, Captain Vere necessarily appearing as the sole witness in the case, and as such temporarily sinking his rank, though singularly maintaining it in a matter apparently trivial, namely, that he testified from the ship's weather side, with that object having caused the court to sit on the lee side. Concisely he narrated all that had led up to the catastrophe, omitting nothing in Claggart's accusation and deposing as to the manner in which the prisoner had received it. At this testimony the three officers glanced with no little surprise at Billy Budd, the last man they would have suspected either of the mutinous design alleged by Claggart or the undeniable deed he himself had done. The first lieutenant, taking judicial primacy and turning toward the prisoner, said, "Captain Vere has spoken. Is it or is it not as Captain Vere says?"

In response came syllables not so much impeded in the utterance as might have been anticipated. They were these: "Captain Vere tells the truth. It is just as Captain Vere says, but it is not as the master-at-arms said. I have eaten the King's bread and I am true to the King."

"I believe you, my man," said the witness, his voice indicating a suppressed emotion not otherwise betrayed.

"God will bless you for that, your honor!" not without stammering said Billy, and all but broke down. But immediately he was recalled to self-control by another question, to which with the same emotional difficulty of utterance he said, "No, there was no malice between us. I never bore malice against the master-at-arms. I am sorry that he is dead. I did not mean to kill him. Could I have used my tongue I would not have struck him. But he foully lied to my face and in presence of my captain, and I had to say something, and I could only say it with a blow, God help me!"

In the impulsive aboveboard manner of the frank one the court saw confirmed all that was implied in words that just previously had perplexed them, coming as they did from the testifier to the tragedy and promptly following Billy's impassioned disclaimer of mutinous intent—Captain Vere's words, "I believe you, my man."

Next it was asked of him whether he knew of or suspected aught savoring of incipient trouble (meaning mutiny, though the explicit term was avoided) going on in any section of the ship's company.

The reply lingered. This was naturally imputed by the court to the same vocal embarrassment which had retarded or obstructed previous answers. But in main it was otherwise here, the question immediately recalling to Billy's mind the interview with the afterguardsman in the forechains. But an innate repugnance to playing a part at all approaching that of an informer against one's own shipmates—the same erring sense of uninstructed honor which had stood in the way of his reporting the matter at the time, though as a loyal man-of-war's man it was incumbent on him, and failure so to do, if charged against him and proven, would have subjected him to the heaviest of penalties; this, with the blind feeling now his that nothing really was being hatched, prevailed with him. When the answer came it was a negative.

"One question more," said the officer of marines, now first speaking and with a troubled earnestness. "You tell us that what the master-at-arms said against you was a lie. Now why should he have so lied, so maliciously lied, since you declare there was no malice between you?"

At that question, unintentionally touching on a spiritual sphere wholly obscure to Billy's thoughts, he was nonplussed, evincing a confusion indeed that some observers, such as can readily be imagined, would have construed into involuntary evidence of hidden guilt. Nevertheless, he strove some way to answer, but all at once relinquished the vain endeavor, at the same time turning an appealing glance towards Captain Vere as deeming him his best helper and friend. Captain Vere, who had been seated for a time, rose to his feet, addressing the interrogator. "The question you put to him comes naturally enough. But how can he rightly answer it?—or anybody else, unless indeed it be he who lies within there," designating the compartment where lay the corpse. "But the prone one there will not rise to our summons. In effect, though, as it seems to me, the point you make is hardly material. Quite aside from any conceivable motive actuating the master-at-arms, and irrespective of the provocation to the blow, a martial court must needs in the present case confine its attention to the blow's consequence, which consequence justly is to be deemed not otherwise than as the striker's deed."

This utterance, the full significance of which it was not at all likely that Billy took in, nevertheless caused him to turn a wistful interrogative look toward the speaker, a look in its dumb expressiveness not unlike that which a dog of generous breed might turn upon his master, seeking in his face some elucidation of a previous gesture ambiguous to the canine intelligence. Nor was the same utterance without marked effect upon the three officers, more especially the soldier. Couched in it seemed to them a meaning unanticipated, involving a prejudgment on the speaker's part. It served to augment a mental disturbance previously evident enough.

The soldier once more spoke, in a tone of suggestive dubiety addressing at once his associates and Captain Vere: "Nobody is present—none of the ship's company, I mean—who might shed lateral light, if any is to be had, upon what remains mysterious in this matter."

"That is thoughtfully put," said Captain Vere; "I see your drift. Ay, there is a mystery; but, to use a scriptural phrase, it is a 'mystery of iniquity,' a matter for psychologic theologians to discuss. But what has a military court to do with it? Not to add that for us any possible investigation of it is cut off by the lasting tongue-tie of—him—in yonder," again designating the mortuary stateroom. "The prisoner's deed—with that alone we have to do."

To this, and particularly the closing reiteration, the marine soldier, knowing not how aptly to reply, sadly abstained from saying aught. The first lieutenant, who at the outset had not unnaturally assumed primacy in the court, now overrulingly instructed by a glance from Captain Vere, a glance more effective than words, resumed that primacy. Turning to the prisoner, "Budd," he said, and scarce in equable tones, "Budd, if you have aught further to say for yourself, say it now."

Upon this the young sailor turned another quick glance toward Captain Vere; then, as taking a hint from that aspect, a hint confirming his own instinct that silence was now best, replied to the lieutenant, "I have said all, sir."

The marine—the same who had been the sentinel without the cabin door at the time that the foretopman, followed by the master-at-arms, entered it—he, standing by the sailor throughout these judicial proceedings, was now directed to take him back to the after compartment originally assigned to the prisoner and his custodian. As the twain disappeared from view, the three officers, as partially liberated from some inward constraint associated with Billy's mere presence, simultaneously stirred in their seats. They exchanged looks of troubled indecision, yet feeling that decide they must and without long delay.

For Captain Vere, he for the time stood—unconsciously with his back toward them, apparently in one of his absent fits—gazing out from a sashed porthole to windward upon the monotonous blank of the twilight sea. But the court's silence continuing, broken only at moments by brief consultations, in low earnest tones, this served to arouse him and energize him. Turning, he to-and-fro paced the cabin athwart; in the returning ascent to windward climbing the slant deck in the ship's lee roll, without knowing it symbolizing thus in his action a mind resolute to surmount difficulties even if against primitive instincts strong as the wind and the sea. Presently he came to a stand before the three. After scanning their faces he stood less as mustering his thoughts for expression than as one inly deliberating how best to put them to well-meaning men not intellectually mature, men with whom it was necessary to demonstrate certain principles that were axioms to himself. Similar impatience as to talking is perhaps one reason that deters some minds from addressing any popular assemblies.

When speak he did, something, both in the substance of what he said and his manner of saying it, showed the influence of unshared studies modifying and tempering the practical training of an active career. This, along with his phraseology, now and then was suggestive of the grounds whereon rested that imputation of a certain pedantry socially alleged against him by certain naval men of wholly practical cast, captains who nevertheless would frankly concede that His Majesty's navy mustered no more efficient officer of their grade than Starry Vere.

What he said was to this effect: "Hitherto I have been but the witness, little more; and I should hardly think now to take another tone, that of your coadjutor for the time, did I not perceive in you—at the crisis too—a troubled hesitancy, proceeding, I doubt not, from the clash of military duty with moral scruple—scruple vitalized by compassion. For the compassion, how can I otherwise than share it? But, mindful of paramount obligations, I strive against scruples that may tend to enervate decision. Not, gentlemen, that I hide from myself that the case is an exceptional one. Speculatively regarded, it well might be referred to a jury of casuists.[2] But for us here, acting not as casuists or moralists, it is a case practical, and under martial law practically to be dealt with.

"But your scruples: do they move as in a dusk? Challenge them. Make them advance and declare themselves. Come now; do they import something like this: If, mindless of palliating circumstances, we are bound to regard the death of the master-at-arms as the prisoner's deed, then does that deed constitute a capital crime whereof the penalty is a mortal one. But in natural justice is nothing but the prisoner's overt act to be considered? How can we adjudge to summary and shameful death a fellow creature innocent before God, and whom we feel to be so?—Does that state it aright? You sign sad assent. Well, I too feel that, the full force of that. It is Nature. But do these buttons that we wear attest that our allegiance is to Nature? No, to the King. Though the ocean, which is inviolate Nature primeval, though this be the element where we move and have our being as sailors, yet as the King's officers lies our duty in a sphere correspondingly natural? So little is that true, that in receiving our commissions we in the most important regards ceased to be natural free agents. When war is declared are we the commissioned fighters previously consulted? We fight at command. If our judgments approve the war, that is but coincidence. So in other particulars. So now. For suppose condemnation to follow these present proceedings. Would it be so much we ourselves that would condemn as it would be martial law operating through us? For that law and the rigor of it, we are not responsible. Our vowed responsibility is in this: That however pitilessly that law may operate in any instances, we nevertheless adhere to it and administer it.

"But the exceptional in the matter moves the hearts within you. Even so too is mine moved. But let not warm hearts betray heads that should be cool. Ashore in a criminal case, will an upright judge allow himself off the bench to be waylaid by some tender kinswoman of the accused seeking to touch him with her tearful plea? Well, the heart here, sometimes the feminine in man, is as that piteous woman, and hard though it be, she must here be ruled out."

He paused, earnestly studying them for a moment; then resumed.

"But something in your aspect seems to urge that it is not solely the heart that moves in you, but also the conscience, the private conscience. But tell me whether or not, occupying the position we do, private conscience should not yield to that imperial one formulated in the code under which alone we officially proceed?"

Here the three men moved in their seats, less convinced than agitated by the course of an argument troubling but the more the spontaneous conflict within.

Perceiving which, the speaker paused for a moment; then abruptly changing his tone, went on.

"To steady us a bit, let us recur to the facts.—In wartime at sea a man-of-war's man strikes his superior in grade, and the blow kills. Apart from its effect the blow itself is, according to the Articles of War,[3] a capital crime. Furthermore—"

"Ay, sir," emotionally broke in the officer of marines, "in one sense it was. But surely Budd purposed neither mutiny nor homicide."

"Surely not, my good man. And before a court less arbitrary and more merciful than a martial one, that plea would largely extenuate. At the Last Assizes[4] it shall acquit. But how here? We proceed under the law of the Mutiny Act.[5] In feature no child can resemble his father more than that Act resembles in spirit the thing from which it derives—War. In His Majesty's service—in this ship, indeed—there are Englishmen forced to fight for the King against their will. Against their conscience, for aught we know. Though as their fellow creatures some of us may appreciate their position, yet as navy officers what reck we of it? Still less recks the enemy. Our impressed men he would fain cut down in the same swath with our volunteers. As regards the enemy's naval conscripts, some of whom may even share our own abhorrence of the regicidal French Directory, it is the same on our side. War looks but to the frontage, the appearance. And the Mutiny Act, War's child, takes after the father. Budd's intent or nonintent is nothing to the purpose.

"But while, put to it by those anxieties in you which I cannot but respect, I only repeat myself—while thus strangely we prolong proceedings that should be summary—the enemy may be sighted and an engagement result. We must do; and one of two things must we do—condemn or let go."

"Can we not convict and yet mitigate the penalty?" asked the sailing master, here speaking, and falteringly, for the first.

"Gentlemen, were that clearly lawful for us under the circumstances, consider the consequences of such clemency. The people" (meaning the ship's company) "have native sense; most of them are familiar with our naval usage and tradition; and how would they take it? Even could you explain to them—which our official position forbids—they, long molded by arbitrary discipline, have not that kind of intelligent responsiveness that might qualify them to comprehend and discriminate. No, to the people the foretopman's deed, however it be worded in the announcement, will be plain homicide committed in a flagrant act of mutiny. What penalty for that should follow, they know. But it does not follow. *Why?* they will ruminate. You know what sailors are. Will they not revert to the recent outbreak at the Nore? Ay. They know the well-founded alarm—the panic it struck throughout England. Your clement sentence they would account pusillanimous. They would think that we flinch, that we are afraid of them—afraid of practicing a lawful rigor singularly demanded at this juncture, lest it should provoke new troubles. What shame to us such a conjecture on their part, and how deadly to discipline. You see then, whither, prompted by duty and the law, I steadfastly drive. But I beseech you, my friends, do not take me amiss. I feel as you do for this unfortunate boy. But did he know our hearts, I take him to be of that generous nature that he would feel even for us on whom in this military necessity so heavy a compulsion is laid."

With that, crossing the deck he resumed his place by the sashed porthole, tacitly leaving the three to come to a decision. On the cabin's opposite side the troubled court sat silent. Loyal lieges, plain and practical, though at bottom they dissented from some points Captain Vere had put to them, they were without the faculty, hardly had the inclination, to gainsay one whom they felt to be an earnest man, one too not less their superior in mind than in naval rank. But it is not improbable that even such of his words as were not without influence over them, less came home to them than his closing appeal to their instinct as sea officers: in the forethought he threw out as to the practical consequences to discipline, considering the unconfirmed tone of the fleet at the time, should a man-of-war's man's violent killing at sea of a superior in grade be allowed to pass for aught else than a capital crime demanding prompt infliction of the penalty.

Not unlikely they were brought to something more or less akin to that harassed frame of mind which in the year 1842 actuated the commander of the U.S. brig-of-war *Somers*[6] to resolve, under the so-called Articles of War, Articles modeled upon the English Mutiny Act, to resolve upon the execution at sea of a midshipman and two sailors as mutineers designing the seizure of the brig. Which resolution was carried out though in a time of peace and within not many days' sail of home. An act vindicated by a naval court of inquiry subsequently convened ashore. History, and here cited without comment. True, the circumstances on board the *Somers* were different from those on board the *Bellipotent*. But the urgency felt, well-warranted or otherwise, was much the same.

Says a writer whom few know,[7] "Forty years after a battle it is easy for a noncombatant to reason about how it ought to have been fought. It is another thing personally and under fire to have to direct the fighting while involved in the obscuring smoke of it. Much so with respect to other emergencies involving considerations both practical and moral, and when it is imperative promptly to act. The greater the fog the more it imperils the steamer, and speed is put on though at the hazard of running somebody down. Little ween the snug card players in the cabin of the responsibilities of the sleepless man on the bridge."

In brief, Billy Budd was formally convicted and sentenced to be hung at the yardarm in the early morning watch, it being now night. Otherwise, as is customary in such cases, the sentence would forthwith have been carried out. In wartime on the field or in the fleet, a mortal punishment decreed by a drumhead court—on the field sometimes decreed by but a nod from the general—follows without delay on the heel of conviction, without appeal.

22

IT WAS CAPTAIN VERE HIMSELF who of his own motion communicated the finding of the court to the prisoner, for that purpose going to the compartment where he was in custody and bidding the marine there to withdraw for the time.

Beyond the communication of the sentence, what took place at this interview was never known. But in view of the character of the twain briefly closeted in that stateroom, each radically sharing in the rarer qualities of our nature—so rare indeed as to be all but incredible to average minds however much cultivated—some conjectures may be ventured.

It would have been in consonance with the spirit of Captain Vere should he on this occasion have concealed nothing from the condemned one—should he indeed have frankly disclosed to him the part he himself had played in bringing about the decision, at the same time revealing his actuating motives. On Billy's side it is not improbable that such a confession would have been received in much the same spirit that prompted it. Not without a sort of joy, indeed, he might have appreciated the brave opinion of him implied in his captain's making such a confidant of him. Nor, as to the sentence itself, could he have been insensible that it was imparted to him as to one not afraid to die. Even more may have been. Captain Vere in end may have developed the passion sometimes latent under an exterior stoical or indifferent. He was old enough to have been Billy's father. The austere devotee of military duty, letting himself melt back into what remains primeval in our formalized humanity, may in end have caught Billy to his heart, even as Abraham may have caught young Isaac on the brink of resolutely offering him up in obedience to the exacting behest.[1] But there is no telling the sacrament, seldom if in any case revealed to the gadding world, wherever under circumstances at all akin to those here attempted to be set forth two of great Nature's nobler order embrace. There is privacy at the time, inviolable to the survivor; and holy oblivion, the sequel to each diviner magnanimity, providentially covers all at last.

The first to encounter Captain Vere in act of leaving the compartment was the senior lieutenant. The face he beheld, for the moment one expressive of the agony of the strong, was to that officer, though a man of fifty, a startling revelation. That the condemned one suffered less than he who mainly had effected the condemnation was apparently indicated by the former's exclamation in the scene soon perforce to be touched upon.

23

O F A SERIES OF INCIDENTS within a brief term rapidly following each other, the adequate narration may take up a term less brief, especially if explanation or comment here and there seem requisite to the better understanding of such incidents. Between the entrance into the cabin of him who never left it alive, and him who when he did leave it left it as one condemned to die; between this and the closeted interview just given, less than an hour and a half had elapsed. It was an interval long enough, however, to awaken speculations among no few of the ship's company as to what it was that could be detaining in the cabin the master-at-arms and the sailor, for a rumor that both of them had been seen to enter it and neither of them had been seen to emerge, this rumor had got abroad upon the gun decks and in the tops, the people of a great warship being in one respect like villagers, taking microscopic note of every outward movement or nonmovement going on. When therefore, in weather not at all tempestuous, all hands were called in the second dogwatch, a summons under such circumstances not usual in those hours, the crew were not wholly unprepared for some announcement extraordinary, one having connection too with the continued absence of the two men from their wonted haunts.

There was a moderate sea at the time; and the moon, newly risen and near to being at its full, silvered the white spar deck wherever not blotted by the clear-cut shadows horizontally thrown, of fixtures and moving men. On either side the quarter-deck the marine guard under arms was drawn up; and Captain Vere, standing in his place surrounded by all the wardroom officers, addressed his men. In so doing, his manner showed neither more nor less than that properly pertaining to his supreme position aboard his own ship. In clear terms and concise he told them what had taken place in the cabin: that the master-at-arms was dead, that he who had killed him had been already tried by a summary court and condemned to death, and that the execution would take place in the early morning watch. The word *mutiny* was not named in what he said. He refrained too from making the occasion an opportunity for any preachment as to the maintenance of discipline, thinking perhaps that under existing circumstances in the navy the consequence of violating discipline should be made to speak for itself.

Their captain's announcement was listened to by the throng of standing sailors in a dumbness like that of a seated congregation of believers in hell listening to the clergyman's announcement of his Calvinistic text.

At the close, however, a confused murmur went up. It began to wax. All but instantly, then, at a sign, it was pierced and suppressed by shrill whistles of the boatswain and his mates. The word was given to about ship.

To be prepared for burial Claggart's body was delivered to certain petty officers of his mess. And here, not to clog the sequel with lateral matters, it may be added that at a suitable hour, the master-at-arms was committed to the sea with every funeral honor properly belonging to his naval grade.

In this proceeding as in every public one growing out of the tragedy strict adherence to usage was observed. Nor in any point could it have been at all deviated from, either with respect to Claggart or Billy Budd, without begetting undesirable speculations in the ship's company, sailors, and more particularly men-of-war's men, being of all men the greatest sticklers for usage. For similar cause, all communication between Captain Vere and the condemned one ended with the closeted interview already given, the latter being now surrendered to the ordinary routine preliminary to the end. His transfer under guard from the captain's quarters was effected without unusual precautions—at least no visible ones. If possible, not to let the men so much as surmise that their officers anticipate aught amiss from them is the tacit rule in a military ship. And the more that some sort of trouble should really be apprehended, the more do the officers keep that apprehension to themselves, though not the less unostentatious vigilance may be augmented. In the present instance, the sentry placed over the prisoner had strict orders to let no one have communication with him but the chaplain. And certain unobtrusive measures were taken absolutely to insure this point.

24

IN A SEVENTY-FOUR of the old order the deck known as the upper gun deck was the one covered over by the spar deck, which last, though not without its armament, was for the most part exposed to the weather. In general it was at all hours free from hammocks; those of the crew swinging on the lower gun deck and berth deck, the latter being not only a dormitory but also the place for the stowing of the sailors' bags, and on both sides lined with the large chests or movable pantries of the many messes of the men.

On the starboard side of the *Bellipotent*'s upper gun deck, behold Billy Budd under sentry lying prone in irons in one of the bays formed by the regular spacing of the guns comprising the batteries on either side. All these pieces were of the heavier caliber of that period. Mounted on lumbering wooden carriages, they were hampered with cumbersome harness of breeching and strong side-tackles for running them out. Guns and carriages, together with the long rammers and shorter lin-stocks lodged in loops overhead—all these, as customary, were painted black; and the heavy hempen breechings, tarred to the same tint, wore the like livery of the undertakers. In contrast with the funereal hue of these surroundings, the prone sailor's exterior apparel, white jumper and white duck trousers, each more or less soiled, dimly glimmered in the obscure light of the bay like a patch of discolored snow in early April lingering at some upland cave's black mouth. In effect he is already in his shroud, or the garments that shall serve him in lieu of one. Over him but scarce illuminating him, two battle lanterns swing from two massive beams of the deck above. Fed with the oil supplied by the war contractors (whose gains, honest or otherwise, are in every land an anticipated portion of the harvest of death), with flickering splashes of dirty yellow light they pollute the pale moonshine all but ineffectually struggling in obstructed flecks through the open ports from which the tampioned cannon protrude. Other lanterns at intervals serve but to bring out somewhat the obscurer bays which, like small confessionals or side-chapels in a cathedral, branch from the long dim-vistaed broad aisle between the two batteries of that covered tier.

Such was the deck where now lay the Handsome Sailor. Through the rose-tan of his complexion no pallor could have shown. It would have taken days of sequestration from the winds and the sun to have brought about the effacement of that. But the skeleton in the cheekbone at the point of its angle was just beginning delicately to be defined under the warm-tinted skin. In fervid hearts self-contained, some brief experiences devour our human tissue as secret fire in a ship's hold consumes cotton in the bale.

But now lying between the two guns, as nipped in the vice of fate, Billy's agony, mainly proceeding from a generous young heart's virgin experience of the diabolical incarnate and effective in some men—the tension of that agony was over now. It survived not the something healing in the closeted interview with Captain Vere. Without movement, he lay as in a trance, that adolescent expression previously noted as his taking on something akin to the look of a slumbering child in the cradle when the warm hearth-glow of the still chamber at night plays on the dimples that at whiles mysteriously form in the cheek, silently coming and going there. For now and then in the gyved one's trance a serene happy light born of some wandering reminiscence or dream would diffuse itself over his face, and then wane away only anew to return.

The chaplain, coming to see him and finding him thus, and perceiving no sign that he was conscious of his presence, attentively regarded him for a space, then slipping aside, withdrew for the time, peradventure feeling that even he, the minister of Christ though receiving his stipend from Mars,[1] had no consolation to proffer which could result in a peace transcending that which he beheld. But in the small hours he came again. And the prisoner, now awake to his surroundings, noticed his approach, and civilly, all but cheerfully, welcomed him. But it was to little purpose that in the interview following, the good man sought to bring Billy Budd to some godly understanding that he must die, and at dawn. True, Billy himself freely referred to his death as a thing close at hand; but it was something in the way that children will refer to death in general, who yet among their other sports will play a funeral with hearse and mourners.

Not that like children Billy was incapable of conceiving what death really is. No, but he was wholly without irrational fear of it, a fear more prevalent in highly civilized communities than those so-called barbarous ones which in all respects stand nearer to unadulterate Nature. And, as elsewhere said, a barbarian Billy radically was—as much so, for all the costume, as his countrymen the British captives, living trophies, made to march in the Roman triumph of Germanicus.[2] Quite as much so as those later barbarians, young men probably, and picked specimens among the earlier British converts to Christianity, at least nominally such, taken to Rome (as today converts from lesser isles of the sea may be taken to London), of whom the Pope of that time,[3] admiring the strangeness of their personal beauty so unlike the Italian stamp, their clear ruddy complexion and curled flaxen locks, exclaimed, "Angles" (meaning *English,* the modern derivative), "Angles, do you call them? And is it because they look so like angels?" Had it been later in time, one would think that the Pope had in mind Fra Angelico's seraphs,[4] some of whom, plucking apples in gardens of the Hesperides,[5] have the faint rosebud complexion of the more beautiful English girls.

If in vain the good chaplain sought to impress the young barbarian with ideas of death akin to those conveyed in the skull, dial, and crossbones on old tombstones, equally futile to all appearance were his efforts to bring home to him the thought of salvation and a Savior. Billy listened, but less out of awe or reverence, perhaps, than from a certain natural politeness, doubtless at bottom regarding all that in much the same way that most mariners of his class take any discourse abstract or out of the common tone of the workaday world. And this sailor way of taking clerical discourse is not wholly unlike the way in which the primer of Christianity, full of transcendent miracles, was received long ago on tropic isles by any superior *savage,* so called—a Tahitian, say, of Captain Cook's[6] time or shortly after that time. Out of natural courtesy he received, but did not appropriate. It was like a gift placed in the palm of an outreached hand upon which the fingers do not close.

But the *Bellipotent*'s chaplain was a discreet man possessing the good sense of a good heart. So he insisted not in his vocation here. At the instance of Captain Vere, a lieutenant had apprised him of pretty much everything as to Billy; and since he felt that innocence was even a better thing than religion wherewith to go to Judgment, he reluctantly withdrew; but in his emotion not without first performing an act strange enough in an Englishman, and under the circumstances yet more so in any regular priest. Stooping over, he kissed on the fair cheek his fellow man, a felon in martial law, one whom though on the confines of death he felt he could never convert to a dogma; nor for all that did he fear for his future.

Marvel not that having been made acquainted with the young sailor's essential innocence the worthy man lifted not a finger to avert the doom of such a martyr to martial discipline. So to do would not only have been as idle as invoking the desert, but would also have been an audacious transgression of the bounds of his function, one as exactly prescribed to him by military law as that of the boatswain or any other naval officer. Bluntly put, a chaplain is the minister of the Prince of Peace serving in the host of the God of War—Mars. As such, he is as incongruous as a musket would be on the altar at Christmas. Why, then, is he there? Because he indirectly subserves the purpose attested by the cannon; because too he lends the sanction of the religion of the meek to that which practically is the abrogation of everything but brute Force.

25

THE NIGHT SO LUMINOUS on the spar deck, but otherwise on the cavernous ones below, levels so like the tiered galleries in a coal mine—the luminous night passed away. But like the prophet in the chariot disappearing in heaven and dropping his mantle to Elisha,[1] the withdrawing night transferred its pale robe to the breaking day. A meek, shy light appeared in the East, where stretched a diaphanous fleece of white furrowed vapor. That light slowly waxed. Suddenly *eight bells* was struck aft, responded to by one louder metallic stroke from forward. It was four o'clock in the morning. Instantly the silver whistles were heard summoning all hands to witness punishment. Up through the great hatchways rimmed with racks of heavy shot the watch below came pouring, overspreading with the watch already on deck the space between the mainmast and foremast including that occupied by the capacious launch and the black booms tiered on either side of it, boat and booms making a summit of observation for the powder-

113

boys and younger tars. A different group comprising one watch of topmen leaned over the rail of that sea balcony, no small one in a seventy-four, looking down on the crowd below. Man or boy, none spake but in whisper, and few spake at all. Captain Vere—as before, the central figure among the assembled commissioned officers—stood nigh the break of the poop deck facing forward. Just below him on the quarter-deck the marines in full equipment were drawn up much as at the scene of the promulgated sentence.

At sea in the old time, the execution by halter of a military sailor was generally from the foreyard. In the present instance, for special reasons the mainyard was assigned. Under an arm of that yard the prisoner was presently brought up, the chaplain attending him. It was noted at the time, and remarked upon afterwards, that in this final scene the good man evinced little or nothing of the perfunctory. Brief speech indeed he had with the condemned one, but the genuine Gospel was less on his tongue than in his aspect and manner towards him. The final preparations personal to the latter being speedily brought to an end by two boatswain's mates, the consummation impended. Billy stood facing aft. At the penultimate moment, his words, his only ones, words wholly unobstructed in the utterance, were these: "God bless Captain Vere!" Syllables so unanticipated coming from one with the ignominious hemp about his neck—a conventional felon's benediction directed aft towards the quarters of honor; syllables too delivered in the clear melody of a singing bird on the point of launching from the twig—had a phenomenal effect, not unenhanced by the rare personal beauty of the young sailor, spiritualized now through late experiences so poignantly profound.

Without volition, as it were, as if indeed the ship's populace were but the vehicles of some vocal current electric, with one voice from alow and aloft came a resonant sympathetic echo: "God bless Captain Vere!" And yet at that instant Billy alone must have been in their hearts, even as in their eyes.

At the pronounced words and the spontaneous echo that voluminously rebounded them, Captain Vere, either through stoic self-control or a sort of momentary paralysis induced by emotional shock, stood erectly rigid as a musket in the ship-armorer's rack.

The hull, deliberately recovering from the periodic roll to leeward, was just regaining an even keel when the last signal, a preconcerted dumb one, was given. At the same moment it chanced that the vapory fleece hanging low in the East was shot through with a soft glory as of the fleece of the Lamb of God seen in mystical vision,[2] and simultaneously therewith, watched by the wedged mass of upturned faces, Billy ascended; and, ascending, took the full rose of the dawn.[3]

In the pinioned figure arrived at the yard-end, to the wonder of all no motion was apparent, none save that created by the slow roll of the hull in moderate weather, so majestic in a great ship ponderously cannoned.

26

WHEN SOME DAYS AFTERWARDS, in reference to the singularity just mentioned, the purser, a rather ruddy, rotund person more accurate as an accountant than profound as a philosopher, said at mess to the surgeon, "What testimony to the force lodged in will power," the latter, saturnine, spare, and tall, one in whom a discreet causticity went along with a manner less genial than polite, replied, "Your pardon, Mr. Purser. In a hanging scientifically conducted—and under special orders I myself directed how Budd's was to be effected—any movement following the completed suspension and originating in the body suspended, such movement indicates mechanical spasm in the muscular system. Hence the absence of that is no more attributable to will power, as you call it, than to horsepower—begging your pardon."

"But this muscular spasm you speak of, is not that in a degree more or less invariable in these cases?"

"Assuredly so, Mr. Purser."

"How then, my good sir, do you account for its absence in this instance?"

"Mr. Purser, it is clear that your sense of the singularity in this matter equals not mine. You account for it by what you call will power—a term not yet included in the lexicon of science. For me, I do not, with my present knowledge, pretend to account for it at all. Even should we assume the hypothesis that at the first touch of the halyards the action of Budd's heart, intensified by extraordinary emotion at its climax, abruptly stopped—much like a watch when in carelessly winding it up you strain at the finish, thus snapping the chain—even under that hypothesis how account for the phenomenon that followed?"

"You admit, then, that the absence of spasmodic movement was phenomenal."

"It was phenomenal, Mr. Purser, in the sense that it was an appearance the cause of which is not immediately to be assigned."

"But tell me, my dear sir," pertinaciously continued the other, "was the man's death effected by the halter, or was it a species of euthanasia?"[1]

"*Euthanasia*, Mr. Purser, is something like your *will power*: I doubt its authenticity as a scientific term—begging your pardon again. It is at once imaginative and metaphysical—in short, Greek—But," abruptly changing his tone, "there is a case in the sick bay that I do not care to leave to my assistants. Beg your pardon, but excuse me." And rising from the mess he formally withdrew.

27

THE SILENCE at the moment of execution and for a moment or two continuing thereafter, a silence but emphasized by the regular wash of the sea against the hull or the flutter of a sail caused by the helmsman's eyes being tempted astray, this emphasized silence was gradually disturbed by a sound not easily to be verbally rendered. Whoever has heard the freshet-wave of a torrent suddenly swelled by pouring showers in tropical mountains, showers not shared by the plain; whoever has heard the first muffled murmur of its sloping advance through precipitous woods may form some conception of the sound now heard. The seeming remoteness of its source was because of its murmurous indistinctness, since it came from close by, even from the men massed on the ship's open deck. Being inarticulate, it was dubious in significance further than it seemed to indicate some capricious revulsion of thought or feeling such as mobs ashore are liable to, in the present instance possibly implying a sullen revocation on the men's part of their involuntary echoing of Billy's benediction. But ere the murmur had time to wax into clamor it was met by a strategic command, the more telling that it came with abrupt unexpectedness: "Pipe down the starboard watch, Boatswain, and see that they go."

Shrill as the shriek of the sea hawk, the silver whistles of the boatswain and his mates pierced that ominous low sound, dissipating it; and yielding to the mechanism of discipline the throng was thinned by one-half. For the remainder, most of them were set to temporary employments connected with trimming the yards and so forth, business readily to be got up to serve occasion by any officer of the deck.

Now each proceeding that follows a mortal sentence pronounced at sea by a drumhead court is characterized by promptitude not perceptibly merging into hurry, though bordering that. The hammock, the one which had been Billy's bed when alive, having already been ballasted with shot and otherwise prepared to serve for his canvas coffin, the last offices of the sea undertakers, the sailmaker's mates, were now speedily completed. When everything was in readiness a second call for all hands, made necessary by the strategic movement before mentioned, was sounded, now to witness burial.

The details of this closing formality it needs not to give. But when the tilted plank let slide its freight into the sea, a second strange human murmur was heard, blended now with another inarticulate sound proceeding from certain larger seafowl who, their attention having been attracted by the peculiar commotion in the water resulting from the heavy sloped dive of the shotted hammock into the sea, flew screaming to the spot. So near the hull did they come, that the stridor or bony creak of their gaunt double-jointed pinions was audible. As the ship under light airs passed on, leaving the burial spot astern, they still kept circling it low down with the moving shadow of their outstretched wings and the croaked requiem of their cries.

Upon sailors as superstitious as those of the age preceding ours, men-of-war's men too who had just beheld the prodigy of repose in the form suspended in air, and now foundering in the deeps; to such mariners the action of the seafowl, though dictated by mere animal greed for prey, was big with no prosaic significance. An uncertain movement began among them, in which some encroachment was made. It was tolerated but for a moment. For suddenly the drum beat to quarters, which familiar sound happening at least twice every day, had upon the present occasion a signal peremptoriness in it. True martial discipline long continued superinduces in average man a sort of impulse whose operation at the official word of command much resembles in its promptitude the effect of an instinct.

The drumbeat dissolved the multitude, distributing most of them along the batteries of the two covered gun decks. There, as wonted, the guns' crews stood by their respective cannon erect and silent. In due course the first officer, sword under arm and standing in his place on the quarter-deck, formally received the successive reports of the sworded lieutenants commanding the sections of batteries below; the last of which reports being made, the summed report he delivered with the customary salute to the commander. All this occupied time, which in the present case was the object in beating to quarters at an hour prior to the customary one. That such variance from usage was authorized by an officer like Captain Vere, a martinet as some deemed him, was evidence of the necessity for unusual action implied in what he deemed to be temporarily the mood of his men. "With mankind," he would say, "forms, measured forms, are everything; and that is the import couched in the story of Orpheus[1] with his lyre spellbinding the wild denizens of the wood." And this he once applied to the disruption of forms going on across the Channel and the consequences thereof.

At this unwonted muster at quarters, all proceeded as at the regular hour. The band on the quarter-deck played a sacred air, after which the chaplain went through the customary morning service. That done, the drum beat the retreat; and toned by music and religious rites subserving the discipline and purposes of war, the men in their wonted orderly manner dispersed to the places alloted them when not at the guns.

And now it was full day. The fleece of low-hanging vapor had vanished, licked up by the sun that late had so glorified it. And the circumambient air in the clearness of its serenity was like smooth white marble in the polished block not yet removed from the marble-dealer's yard.

28

T**HE SYMMETRY OF FORM** attainable in pure fiction cannot so readily be achieved in a narration essentially having less to do with fable than with fact. Truth uncompromisingly told will always have its ragged edges; hence the conclusion of such a narration is apt to be less finished than an architectural finial.[1]

How it fared with the Handsome Sailor during the year of the Great Mutiny has been faithfully given. But though properly the story ends with his life, something in way of sequel will not be amiss. Three brief chapters will suffice.

In the general rechristening under the Directory of the craft originally forming the navy of the French monarchy, the *St. Louis* line-of-battle ship was named the *Athée* (the *Atheist*). Such a name, like some other substituted ones in the Revolutionary fleet, while proclaiming the infidel audacity of the ruling power, was yet, though not so intended to be, the aptest name, if one consider it, ever given to a warship; far more so indeed

122

than the *Devastation*, the *Erebus* (the *Hell*), and similar names bestowed upon fighting ships.

On the return passage to the English fleet from the detached cruise during which occurred the events already recorded, the *Bellipotent* fell in with the *Athée*. An engagement ensued, during which Captain Vere, in the act of putting his ship alongside the enemy with a view of throwing his boarders across her bulwarks, was hit by a musket ball from a porthole of the enemy's main cabin. More than disabled, he dropped to the deck and was carried below to the same cockpit where some of his men already lay. The senior lieutenant took command. Under him the enemy was finally captured, and though much crippled was by rare good fortune successfully taken into Gibraltar, an English port not very distant from the scene of the fight. There, Captain Vere with the rest of the wounded was put ashore. He lingered for some days, but the end came. Unhappily he was cut off too early for the Nile and Trafalgar. The spirit that 'spite its philosophic austerity may yet have indulged in the most secret of all passions, ambition, never attained to the fullness of fame.

Not long before death, while lying under the influence of that magical drug which, soothing the physical frame, mysteriously operates on the subtler element in man, he was heard to murmur words inexplicable to his attendant: "Billy Budd, Billy Budd." That these were not the accents of remorse would seem clear from what the attendant said to the *Bellipotent*'s senior officer of marines, who, as the most reluctant to condemn of the members of the drumhead court, too well knew, though here he kept the knowledge to himself, who Billy Budd was.

29

SOME FEW WEEKS after the execution, among other matters under the head of "News from the Mediterranean," there appeared in a naval chronicle of the time, an authorized weekly publication, an account of the affair.[1] It was doubtless for the most part written in good faith, though the medium, partly rumor, through which the facts must have reached the writer served to deflect and in part falsify them. The account was as follows:

"On the tenth of the last month a deplorable occurrence took place on board H.M.S. *Bellipotent*. John Claggart, the ship's master-at-arms, discovering that some sort of plot was incipient among an inferior section of the ship's company, and that the ringleader was one William Budd; he, Claggart, in the act of arraigning the man before the captain, was vindictively stabbed to the heart by the suddenly drawn sheath knife of Budd.

"The deed and the implement employed sufficiently suggest that though mustered into the service under an English name the assassin was no Englishman, but one of those aliens adopting English cognomens[2] whom the present extraordinary necessities of the service have caused to be admitted into it in considerable numbers.

"The enormity of the crime and the extreme depravity of the criminal appear the greater in view of the character of the victim, a middle-aged man respectable and discreet, belonging to that minor official grade, the petty officers, upon whom, as none know better than the commissioned gentlemen, the efficiency of His Majesty's navy so largely depends. His function was a responsible one, at once onerous and thankless; and his fidelity in it the greater because of his strong patriotic impulse. In this instance as in so many other instances in these days, the character of this unfortunate man signally refutes, if refutation were needed, that peevish saying attributed to the late Dr. Johnson,[3] that patriotism is the last refuge of a scoundrel.

"The criminal paid the penalty of his crime. The promptitude of the punishment has proved salutary. Nothing amiss is now apprehended aboard H.M.S. *Bellipotent.*"

The above, appearing in a publication now long ago superannuated and forgotten, is all that hitherto has stood in human record to attest what manner of men respectively were John Claggart and Billy Budd.

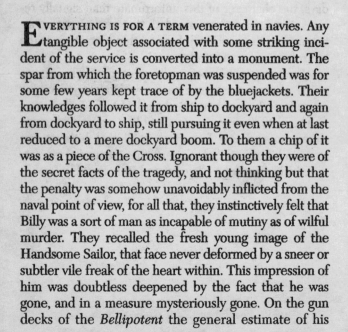

EVERYTHING IS FOR A TERM venerated in navies. Any tangible object associated with some striking incident of the service is converted into a monument. The spar from which the foretopman was suspended was for some few years kept trace of by the bluejackets. Their knowledges followed it from ship to dockyard and again from dockyard to ship, still pursuing it even when at last reduced to a mere dockyard boom. To them a chip of it was as a piece of the Cross. Ignorant though they were of the secret facts of the tragedy, and not thinking but that the penalty was somehow unavoidably inflicted from the naval point of view, for all that, they instinctively felt that Billy was a sort of man as incapable of mutiny as of wilful murder. They recalled the fresh young image of the Handsome Sailor, that face never deformed by a sneer or subtler vile freak of the heart within. This impression of him was doubtless deepened by the fact that he was gone, and in a measure mysteriously gone. On the gun decks of the *Bellipotent* the general estimate of his

nature and its unconscious simplicity eventually found
rude utterance from another foretopman, one of his own
watch, gifted, as some sailors are, with an artless *poetic*
temperament. The tarry hand made some lines which,
after circulating among the shipboard crews for a while,
finally got rudely printed at Portsmouth as a ballad. The
title given to it was the sailor's.

Billy in the Darbies[1]

Good of the chaplain to enter Lone Bay
And down on his marrowbones here and pray
For the likes just o' me, Billy Budd.—But, look:
Through the port comes the moonshine astray!
It tips the guard's cutlass and silvers this nook;
But 'twill die in the dawning of Billy's last day.
A jewel-block they'll make of me tomorrow,
Pendant pearl from the yardarm-end
Like the eardrop I gave to Bristol Molly—
O, 'tis me, not the sentence they'll suspend.
Ay, ay, all is up; and I must up too,
Early in the morning, aloft from alow.
On an empty stomach now never it would do.
They'll give me a nibble—bit o' biscuit ere I go.
Sure, a messmate will reach me the last parting cup;
But, turning heads away from the hoist and the belay,
Heaven knows who will have the running of me up!
No pipe to those halyards.—But aren't it all sham?
A blur's in my eyes; it is dreaming that I am.
A hatchet to my hawser? All adrift to go?
The drum roll to grog, and Billy never know?
But Donald he has promised to stand by the plank;
So I'll shake a friendly hand ere I sink.
But—no! It is dead then I'll be, come to think.

I remember Taff the Welshman when he sank.
And his cheek it was like the budding pink.
But me they'll lash in hammock, drop me deep.
Fathoms down, fathoms down, how I'll dream fast
    asleep.
I feel it stealing now. Sentry, are you there?
Just ease these darbies at the wrist,
And roll me over fair!
I am sleepy, and the oozy weeds about me twist.

NOTES

Title

Billy Budd, Sailor (An Inside Narrative). This title is that of the transcription by Harrison Hayford and Merton M. Sealts, published by the University of Chicago Press in 1962.

Dedication

Jack Chase was one of Melville's shipmates aboard the USS *United States*. He is featured as one of the main characters in *White-Jacket*, a novel Melville published in 1850.

Chapter 1

1. **man-of-war:** A national navy ship armed with between 20 and 120 guns.
2. **Aldebaran:** Most brilliant star in the constellation

Taurus, known in astrology as the second zodiac sign. Those born under this sign are thought to be trustworthy, dependable, and charitable.

3. **Liverpool:** Both Liverpool and the Erie Canal were ports Melville himself visited half a century before this narrative was written.

4. **Ham:** Father of Canaan and third son of Noah. In Genesis (9:18–27), Noah curses Ham's sons and their descendants, a curse Melville's contemporaries used to justify slavery. Melville implies that this racist justification is completely wrong by suggesting that Budd, the modern version of Ham, is not a natural slave and is in fact noble.

5. **Anacharsis Cloots:** Jean-Baptiste du Val-de-Grâce, Baron de Cloots was famous for supporting the French Revolution. He gave himself the titles "Anacharsis" as well as "The Orator of Mankind" and declared himself to be one among the "embassy of the human race" when he addressed the National Assembly in 1791.

6. **pagod:** An idol.

7. **Murat:** Joachim Murat (1767–1815) was one of Napoléon's French cavalry leaders, who became king of Naples in 1808. He was known to be both ambitious and vain, though he was responsible for many progressive reforms in Italy.

8. **Bucephalus:** A fierce horse whose name means "bull-head," Bucephalus was tamed by Alexander the Great of Greece (356–323 B.C.), an act that fulfilled a prophecy made by an oracle.

9. **foretopman:** A sailor positioned at the top of the foremast of a ship. Foretopmen were usually stronger, younger sailors.

10. **impressed:** Forced to serve in the military. Though

during Melville's time it was obsolete, during the late eighteenth century, impressment was a common practice.

11. *Bellipotent:* Powerful in war.

12. *Rights-of-Man:* A document that supported the French Revolution and was published in 1791 by Thomas Paine (1737–1809). Its argument that governments should preserve natural rights directly countered Edmund Burke's (1729–1797) assertion in *Reflections on the French Revolution* (1790) that the natural rights of individuals should be considered subordinate to the government.

13. **Voltaire, Diderot:** Born François-Marie Arouet, Voltaire (1694–1778) wrote literary and philosophical texts aimed at attacking royal authority. Writer Denis Diderot (1713–1784) is considered one of the original philosophers of the Age of Enlightenment.

Chapter 2

1. **bluejackets:** Sailors.

2. **Hercules:** Son of Zeus and Alcmene in Greek mythology, Hercules is known for his strength and fearlessness. He is most often represented in sculpture.

3. *halyards:* Ropes used to raise or lower a sail or flag.

4. **Adam:** Adam is considered the first man in biblical mythology. Melville invokes his name to suggest a loose connection, not a perfect analogy.

5. **doctrine of man's Fall:** Story in Genesis that has Adam tempted by Satan, who takes on the form of a serpent, and then violating God's command to avoid the fruit of the tree of knowledge. God's punishment is exile from the garden of paradise.

6. **Cain's city and citified man:** Cain, oldest son of Adam and Eve, killed his younger brother, Abel, and is banished by God to wander the earth eternally.

7. **Caspar Hauser:** Child of unknown origins (1812–1833) who was found in 1828 in Nuremberg, Germany, and thought to be of noble birth. He was assassinated five years later.

8. **brought?:** Lines written in *Epigrams* by the ancient Roman writer known as Martial, whom many credit as the first to write the modern epigram, or witty, concise saying.

9. **marplot of Eden:** Satan.

Chapter 3

1. **Spithead . . . Nore:** At Spithead, several sailors outraged about their low wages and the abysmal living conditions on board orchestrated a mutiny that lasted from mid-April to mid-May in 1797. The mutineers were able to negotiate a Royal Pardon, a pay raise, and improved living conditions. Just as this mutiny was ending in mid-May, another broke out on the HMS *Sandwich* at Nore, with very different results. These mutineers, led by Richard Parker, protested against their impressment and the poor conditions of nautical military life. Senior officers sent a clear message that what happened at Spithead would not happen again. This mutiny failed miserably; Parker and others were hanged from the yardarm, and others involved were whipped or imprisoned.

2. **France in flames:** Aftereffects of the Reign of Terror (1793–1794).

3. **Red Flag:** Sign of revolution.

4. **Trafalgar:** Admiral Sir Horatio Nelson (1758–1805) is one of England's greatest military heroes, immortalized by his victory at the battle of Trafalgar (1805), during which he received a fatal wound. Vere, the captain of the *Bellipotent,* idolizes him for his loyalty and bravery, though Melville subtly contrasts the two figures.

Chapter 4

1. **Don John . . . 1812:** Don John (1547–1578) was the Austrian naval commander who was victorious over the Turks in the Battle of Lepanto (1571). Andrea Doria (1466–1560) was an Italian admiral who won victories for both France and Spain. Maarten Tromp (1598–1653) was a Dutch commander known as the Father of Naval Tactics, who fought for Britain, France, and Spain. Jean Bart (1650–1702), a French privateer, was known for his courage during his service under King Louis XIV. Stephen Decatur (1779–1820), one of the first American naval heroes, captured a British ship during the War of 1812.

2. *Monitors:* When the Union ship *Monitor* engaged the Confederate *Merrimack,* both innovative iron steam ships, the event marked the emergence of the ironclad, steam-driven warship.

3. **Benthamites of war:** Jeremy Bentham (1748–1832) founded the philosophy of utilitarianism, or the philosophy that actions are moral as long as they benefit the greatest number of people. Melville condemned this belief.

4. *Wellington:* Arthur Wellesley, 1st Duke of Wellington, was a British military commander during the

Napoleonic Wars who later became prime minister of
Great Britain (1828–1830).

5. **Alfred:** Alfred, Lord Tennyson (1809–1892), Poet
   laureate of England (1850–1892), honored Arthur
   Wellesley in the "Ode on the Death of the Duke of
   Wellington" (1852).

Chapter 5

1. **Mansfield:** William Murray, Earl of Mansfield
   (1705–1793), greatly influenced legal policies in
   England and America during his term as lord chief
   justice of Britain.
2. **pennant:** Flag of office.

Chapter 6

1. **De Grasse:** François-Joseph-Paul de Grasse (1722–1788)
   was defeated by British Admiral George Brydges
   Rodney (1718–1792).
2. **Andrew Marvell:** British poet (1621–1678) who
   wrote the poem Melville quotes in this section, titled
   "Lines Upon Appleton House, to My Lord Fairfax," a
   tribute to his benefactor, whose wife's family name
   was Vere.

Chapter 7

1. **Montaigne:** Michel de Montaigne (1533–1592) wrote
   widely revered essays in which he questioned and explored the world around him from his own personal
   opinions and experiences.
2. **journals:** Newspapers.

Chapter 8

1. **Tecumseh:** During the War of 1812, Shawnee warrior Tecumseh (1768?–1813) attempted to unite Indian tribes to fight against American white settlers.
2. **Popish Plot:** A false allegation that Roman Catholics intended to kill Charles II (1630) and terrorize English Protestants made by Reverend Dr. Titus Oates. During the period Oates's story was taken seriously, many Catholics were persecuted or murdered.
3. **phrenologically:** Phrenology was the pseudoscientific study of the shape of a person's skull to determine a person's character.
4. *chevalier:* Con man.
5. **fallen Bastille:** French citizens charged the Bastille fortress, which was being used as a prison, on July 14, 1789, a date that marks the beginning of the French Revolution.
6. **Bunker Hill:** At the battle of Bunker Hill (June 17, 1775), American soldiers bravely fought off British troops. Though they were ultimately forced to surrender at Bunker Hill, the battle is recognized as one of the first major American victories of the American Revolution.
7. **Apocalypse:** End of the world, as it is told in both Testaments of the Bible.

Chapter 9

1. **Dansker:** Dane.
2. **Haden's etching:** Sir Francis Seymour Haden (1818–1910) etched the *Breaking Up of the Agamemnon,* which depicted the demolition of the ninety-one-gun British flagship in 1870.

3. **Merlin:** Legendary wizard of Arthurian romance.
4. **Chiron . . . Achilles:** In Greek mythology, Chiron taught Achilles how to fight, hunt, sing, and play the lyre. He also gave him medical knowledge.

Chapter 10

1. **rattan:** Cane.

Chapter 11

1. *The Mysteries of Udolpho:* This Gothic novel (1794), written by Ann Radcliffe (1764–1823), was one of the most popular works in its day.
2. **honest scholar:** Presumably Melville himself.
3. **Coke and Blackstone:** Sir Edward Coke (1552–1634) and Sir William Blackstone (1723–1780) both profoundly affected the way English law was interpreted.
4. **Natural Depravity:** Melville cites this definition from volume 6 of the Bohn edition (1854).
5. **Calvinism:** Protestant religion led by John Calvin (1509–1564), who believed mankind was corrupt from birth, and whose beliefs Melville did not support.
6. **"mystery of iniquity":** A phrase from 2 Thessalonians 2:7 referring to the unknown nature of evil.

Chapter 12

1. **Chang and Eng:** Siamese congenitally joined twin brothers exhibited at P. T. Barnum's circus in the early- to mid-nineteenth century.
2. **David:** In the famous biblical story, David the shepherd boy defeats the giant Goliath. Saul, father of

David's close friend Jonathan, becomes so jealous he tries to kill David several times.

Chapter 13

1. **Pharisee . . . Fawkes:** Melville unites biblical and historical references here. Jesus condemned the Pharisees for maintaining a pious appearance and upholding civil law but not following God's law; Guy Fawkes (1570–1606) was the most famous conspirator in a plot to bomb Parliament and murder King James I in 1605. For Melville, neither the Pharisees nor Fawkes was capable of remorse.

Chapter 14

1. **Nonconformist:** English Protestant who opposes the Church of England.

Chapter 15

1. **guineas:** Coins.
2. **Delphic:** Ambiguous. In Greek myth, the oracle at Delphi communicates prophecies in unclear language. Melville suggests the Dansker is telling Billy a truth he cannot comprehend completely.

Chapter 17

1. **Hyperion:** A Titan sun god in Greek mythology.
2. **man of sorrows:** Melville quotes from Isaiah 53:3, a reference to Christ.
3. **dental satire of a Guise:** The House of Guise was a

wealthy family who fought for the spread of Roman Catholicism in France, persecuting Protestants in the process.

4. **monomania:** Single-minded obsession.

Chapter 18

1. *genus homo:* A *genus* is a category or grouping; *homo* is the Latin term for man. Melville implies that Budd is an exemplary human.

2. **yardarm-end:** Area of the ship where hangings took place.

3. **Joseph:** Melville emphasizes Claggart's envy by comparing him to the jealous brothers of Joseph, who bring a coat dyed with goat's blood to their father, Jacob, claiming that Joseph has died. Joseph eventually rises to prominence in spite of his brothers' ill treatment.

Chapter 19

1. **suffocation:** In Roman mythology, six priestesses tended Vesta, goddess of the hearth. If they failed to remain virgins, they were suffocated.

2. **Ananias:** Biblical figure who tried to cheat the Apostles but was discovered by Peter.

3. **drumhead court:** An impromptu court, where a drum was sometimes used as a table.

Chapter 21

1. **Peter the Barbarian:** Peter I (1672–1725), first czar of Russia, initiated great progress in his country

but at the expense of repressing his own people. He founded the capital St. Petersburg in 1703.

2. **casuists:** Those who manipulate logic either to rationalize or to deceive.

3. **Articles of War:** Rules followed by the British Royal Navy. Billy is guilty of failing to report information about a possible mutiny under the fourth article. Vere refers, however, to the twenty-second article, which prohibits any type of threat to a superior officer, and the twenty-eighth article, which states that anyone who commits murder must be put to death.

4. **Last Assizes:** An assize is an archaic term used to describe a session of court; Melville uses it to refer to divine judgment.

5. **Mutiny Act:** The English Mutiny Act (1689) evolved into the Articles of War.

6. *Somers:* In November 1842, Captain Alexander Slidell Mackenzie arrested three men under suspicion of arranging a mutiny aboard the USS *Somers*. After consulting a summary court of three officers, one of whom was Melville's cousin Guert Gansevoort, Mackenzie found the men guilty and hanged them. His decision was extremely controversial, as there was never any evidence of guilt.

7. **a writer whom few know:** Presumably Melville himself.

Chapter 22

1. **Abraham . . . behest:** In the Old Testament, God promises Abraham a multitude of descendants but later tests him by requesting that he sacrifice his

son, Isaac. Melville suggests a parallel between this story of patriarchal sacrifice and Vere's sacrifice of Billy.

Chapter 24

1. **Mars:** God of war.
2. **Germanicus:** Germanicus Caesar (15 B.C.–A.D. 19) was a general who helped secure Roman victory in England.
3. **Pope of that time:** Pope Gregory I (540?–604) converted natives of Gaul, Africa, and Northern Italy to Christianity, often by force.
4. **Fra Angelico's seraphs:** Fra Angelico, born Guido di Pietro (1400?–1455), painted some of the most famous religious works in the world. Melville refers to his images of seraphs, or angels of superior rank in medieval lore.
5. **gardens of the Hesperides:** In Greek myth, the Hesperides are the Nymphs of the Setting Sun, three maiden sisters who guarded the apples given to Hera when she married Zeus. Melville refers to *The Garden of the Hesperides*, a painting by Fra Angelico.
6. **Captain Cook:** James Cook (1728–1779) was an English explorer. When he set out in 1768 on the ship *Endeavour*, he discovered the lands now known as Australia and New Zealand for Britain. During that trip, he visited Tahiti in 1769.

Chapter 25

1. **Elisha:** When the prophet Elijah ascends to heaven in a chariot, Elisha inherits his mantle, or role.

2. **mystical vision:** Melville evokes biblical images of
   Christ in his description of Budd's death. In the New
   Testament, John the Baptist declares of Jesus "Behold, the Lamb of God, who takes away the sin of the
   world" (John 1:29), and that he "saw the Spirit come
   down like a dove from the sky and remain upon him"
   (John 1:32). In the Book of Revelation, Christ is a lu-
   minescent figure: "The hair of his head was as white
   as white wool or as snow, and his eyes were like a fiery
   flame" (1:14).

3. **rose of the dawn:** Melville further suggests a parallel between Billy and Christ, as this passage echoes
   the biblical description of Jesus' ascension into heaven.

Chapter 26

1. **euthanasia:** Although euthanasia in contemporary
   culture refers to the controversial act of medically as-
   sisted suicide, Melville uses it here to mean peaceful
   death, from the ancient Greek term *eu thanatos*.

Chapter 27

1. **story of Orpheus:** According to Greek legend, when
   Orpheus loses his wife, Eurydice, he travels to Hades,
   king of the Underworld, to appeal for her life. Hades
   is so enchanted by Orpheus's music that he releases
   Eurydice on the condition that Orpheus not look back
   as he leads Eurydice out of the Underworld. When
   Orpheus turns to look at his wife, she disappears back
   into the Underworld.

Chapter 28

1. **architectural finial:** A finial is an ornamental decoration at the top of a pillar.

Chapter 29

1. **account of the affair:** Though there was a periodical called *The Naval Chronicle*, published regularly from 1799 to 1818, there is no section titled "News from the Mediterranean." Melville uses this as a literary device to show how news misrepresents and simplifies events to suit social and political ideologies.
2. **cognomens:** Cognomen is a term that describes both a surname and a nickname that describes the character.
3. **Dr. Johnson:** Samuel Johnson (1709–1784) was one of the most prolific English writers of the eighteenth century. Melville draws this saying from James Boswell's *The Life of Samuel Johnson, LL.D.* (1791).

Chapter 30

1. **Billy in the Darbies:** This ballad is the original version of the story, a poem Melville wrote in the 1880s from Budd's point of view. "Darbies" is an outdated term for chains.

INTERPRETIVE NOTES

The Plot

It is the summer of 1797. British naval commanders are disturbed by the news that mutinies have just occurred on two of their ships. The young and innocent Billy Budd is involuntarily forced to leave the merchant ship aptly called the *Rights-of-Man* to serve on the British naval ship HMS *Bellipotent*. Captain Graveling is distraught to see Billy Budd depart, as he had played an integral part on the *Rights-of-Man* as peacemaker. Lieutenant Ratcliffe is pleased to acquire the obedient and eager Budd for the *Bellipotent*.

On board the *Bellipotent*, Budd recoils in horror when he witnesses the flogging punishment of a shipmate who had disobeyed orders. Though he resolves to do whatever he can to avoid any reprimand, he finds himself getting in trouble for minor mistakes and is verbally threatened by one of the officers. A veteran, known as the Dansker, gives Budd an ominous though ambiguous warning about the master-at-arms, John Claggart. Budd begins to reflect on the Dansker's warning after perceiving signs that Claggart is against him. Claggart brings his complaints about Budd to Captain Vere, who summons Budd to explain himself. Their meeting ends tragically, and Vere is left with the dilemma of whether to do what is right or to follow the law. Vere makes a controversial choice that determines not only Budd's fate but also his legacy. A news chronicle simplifies and misrepresents what has happened, and a poem mythologizes Budd's story.

Characters

Narrator. The narrator is one of the most complex characters in *Billy Budd*. He is like Melville in that he is experienced both as a writer and as a sailor and was even in Liverpool half a century before the story was composed, as the second paragraph relates. And yet he is not Melville but is rather a character with his own impressions, the insider to whom the subtitle of the novella refers. He finds himself on tangents at times, and forces himself to return to the story. He provides details of certain events but deprives readers of others, most notably the final meeting between Budd and Vere. And finally, he often comments on his own narrative as if Melville is reminding readers that they are reading his version of events.

Billy Budd (Handsome Sailor, Baby Budd). Billy Budd is the twenty-one-year-old foretopman who is impressed, or involuntarily enlisted, into the British Navy, to serve on the HMS *Bellipotent*. Budd is a mysterious figure with no discernible past, but the narrator assumes he has a noble lineage. He is blue-eyed and has features that would have been considered aristocratic. The narrator compares him to the Greek god Hercules, Adam of the Old Testament, and even suggests that he is a Christ-like figure. The one thing that makes him an unconventional hero is that he has a speech impediment.

Lieutenant Ratcliffe. Lieutenant Ratcliffe forces his way onto the *Rights-of-Man* and departs with Budd. He signifies the power the military officers have over others at sea in his commanding and disrespectful behavior during his meeting with Captain Graveling.

Captain Graveling. Shipmaster of the *Rights-of-Man*, Captain Graveling is distressed to lose his favorite sailor, Budd, whom he regards as the peacemaker on his ship. The narrator declares that Graveling is admirable, honest, and exceptionally responsible.

Red Whiskers. Red Whiskers is Captain Graveling's nickname for a red-haired bearded sailor on the *Rights-of-Man* who provokes a conflict with Budd. His aversion to Budd turns into admiration when Budd defends himself.

Captain the Honorable Edward Fairfax Vere (Starry Vere). Captain Vere, an admirable leader who thinks philosophically and acts judiciously, commands the *Bellipotent*. He is in his forties and prefers history, biography, and philosophy to fiction. His men feel that he is austere and doctrinaire, or determined to act according to his own theories and unlikely to consider other approaches.

John Claggart (Jemmy Legs). The thirty-five-year-old master-at-arms of the *Bellipotent*, Claggart is charged with keeping order on the ship as a figurative chief of police. He has black curly hair and is very tall, though his small hands bear no signs of heavy labor. Like Budd, Claggart has no known past, though there were several uncomplimentary rumors about him. If Budd represents innocence, Claggart stands for an inexplicable evil, as the narrator compares him to Satan several times.

The Dansker (Board-Her-in-the-Smoke). The Dansker is a mysterious figure who warns Budd repeatedly about the threat Claggart poses. He is old and wrinkled, and bears the signs of being in battle several times. Two years before this story takes place, he served under Nelson on the *Agamemnon*. He likes Budd for his consistent signs of respect in the form of deferential salutations, though he helps Budd only through cryptic messages.

Squeak. Squeak is a corporal on the *Bellipotent* who relates gossip about Budd to Claggart. The sailors give him his nickname because his high-pitched voice and behavior remind them of a rat.

An Afterguardsman. A stranger who visits Budd during the night once and offers him two guineas if he will join others who are bitter about their impressment. The day after the meeting, Budd thinks he identifies this stranger, though he cannot be sure exactly who it is.

Red Pepper. A red-haired forecastleman Budd encounters after his meeting with the afterguardsman. He expresses disdain for the afterguardsman when Budd tells him about the incident.

Albert. Assistant to Captain Vere as a hammock-boy or sea valet, Albert is Captain Vere's confidant.

The Surgeon. The surgeon is the general doctor on board the *Bellipotent*. He plays an important role in interpreting the tragic events of the novella.

The First Lieutenant. One of the three judges on the drumhead court, the first lieutenant questions Budd at his trial and believes he is innocent after he hears his first response.

Mr. Mordant. Mordant is the captain of the marines and serves as one of the three judges on the drumhead court. Vere admires him for his simplicity but is unsure he can give sound advice.

The Sailing Master. The sailing master is one of the three judges on the drumhead court. He speaks during the trial only to ask if Budd's punishment can be modified.

The Chaplain. The chaplain visits Budd toward the end of the novella and is distraught that he cannot console Budd, who does not grasp his Christian message.

The Purser. The purser is the paymaster on the *Bellipotent*.

Major Themes

The Individual and Society. On several levels, *Billy Budd* is about the relation between the individual and society. Even the names Melville chooses for his fictional ships symbolize the gulf between philosophies regarding that relation. Budd's transfer from the *Rights-of-Man*, named after Thomas Paine's famous text in which he argues that individual rights should supersede institutional power, to the *Bellipotent*, which means "powerful in war," symbolizes his crossing from the world of natural rights to the world of martial law. In this world aboard the *Bellipotent*, preserving social order is more important than considering the rights of the men as individuals. Anyone acting against that order must be punished as an example to the other men. Vere feels that he must show that no form of insurrection will be tolerated on his ship. But Melville emphasizes the subjectivity of Vere's decision by having the narrator question his sanity. Even the members of the court he assembles disagree with his verdict and ask whether there is another solution to his dilemma. Ignoring his individual instincts, Vere adheres to the social law and assumes the role of executioner he believes his job calls him to play, a role that only reenacts the crime it punishes.

The Ethics of Punishment by Death. Though capital punishment was largely unquestioned and frequently practiced during the eighteenth century, it was the subject of fierce debates during the time Melville was writing *Billy Budd* in the late nineteenth century. In his story, Melville invents a story that radically questions the ethics of capital punishment. He implies that other forms of punishment can be just as effective. When Budd sees a shipmate whipped for being absent from his post, for example, "Billy was horrified. He resolved that never through remissness would he make himself liable to such a visitation or do or omit aught that might merit even verbal reproof." By detailing Budd's extreme reaction to a more simple reprimand, Melville subtly suggests that Vere can keep order without capital punishment. Rather than deterring mutiny in the story, capital punishment incites a hum of rebellion that is quickly quelled, but that clearly exists as a menacing threat just below the surface of interactions between the soldiers and their superiors. In the end, rather than preventing crime, capital punishment here has created a hero out of the convict.

The Failure of Language. Several times during the narrative of *Billy Budd*, Melville calls attention to the failure of language. On a literal level, several characters cannot express themselves adequately. Budd's tragic flaw is his speech deficiency. But when he does speak, he is often misunderstood. For example, when he verbally salutes the *Rights-of-Man*, he cries out "And good-bye to you too, old *Rights-of-Man*," an accurate statement given his impressment. The narrator not only assures us that the senior officers all thought it was a sarcastic remark, but also that Budd can neither express nor understand sarcasm. When the Dansker tries to warn Budd about the threat Claggart poses, he stops short of explaining his curt messages. Claggart avoids the term "impressed," and Captain Vere cannot utter the term "mutiny." And of course, in the dramatic climax of the story, Budd's speech impediment causes tragic results.

On a more figurative level, the narrative itself is in question, as the narrator frequently wanders from his topic, admits he has trouble describing elements of the story, and at times refuses to relate parts of it. His first description of the black Handsome Sailor spins off into so many allusions and analogies that he must begin his third paragraph: "To return." When he tries to describe the villainous Claggart, the narrator falters: "His portrait I essay, but shall never hit it." On the subject of whether or not Vere was acting rationally when he judged Budd, the narrator equivocally declares that "every one must determine for himself by such light as this narrative may afford," but Melville has reminded readers that no narrative is perfect. When the captain meets with Budd privately, the narrator states "what took place at this interview was never known," though he also asserts that "some conjectures may be ventured," and then goes on to hypothesize about what must have happened. In a work of nonfiction, this guessing would make sense; in fiction, however, it calls attention to the episode and to other themes that resonate with narrative speculation. Here, the authority of narrative, specifically as history, is radically destabilized.

Finally, the last three chapters illustrate the unreliability of the official social language by which we form our identities: history. The narrator claims that this narrative cannot be symmetrical because this story is "Truth uncompromisingly told," and because it is true, it "will always have its ragged edges." And yet we know that this is a work of fiction, and that Melville has the freedom to end his story any way he decides to end it. The final "naval chronicle," then, distorts the story even as Melville suggests it may never be told properly. A poem—and not the narrator's voice—is what concludes the story, which ends in a haze of indirection and analogy, from the point of view of one of the soldiers. Rather than providing answers and a sense of completion, this poem leaves readers with the questions raised in the narrative, eternal questions about language and what it can and cannot represent.

CRITICAL EXCERPTS

Early Assessments

Murry, John Middleton. "Herman Melville's Silence." *Times Literary Supplement* 1173 (1924).

When *Billy Budd* was published in 1924, more than thirty years after Melville's death, many critics were astonished to find a text as complex and worthy of praise as his masterpiece, *Moby-Dick*. One of those reviewers, John Middleton Murry, was partly responsible for the intense revival of interest in Melville in the 1920s. Originally published anonymously in the *Times Literary Supplement*, this review appeared the same year in the *New York Times Book Review* with Murry's name and the title "Herman Melville, Who Could Not Surpass Himself / Complete Works of a Writer of Colossal Vision— after 'Moby Dick' He Had Nothing More to Say." In this review, Murry wonders why Melville wrote no prose for several years. Though he cannot answer that question, he declares that *Billy Budd* is worth that lengthy silence.

The silence of a writer who has the vision that Melville proved his own in *Moby Dick* is not an accident without adequate cause; and that we feel that silence was the appropriate epilogue to Melville's masterpiece is only the form of our instinctive recognition that adequate cause was there. After *Moby Dick* there was, in a sense, nothing to be said, just as after *King Lear* there seemed nothing for Shakespeare to say. . . . How much [Melville] struggled with his dumbness we cannot say; perhaps during most of those thirty-five years he acquiesced in it. But something was at the back of his mind, haunting him, and this something he could not utter. . . . [Through *Billy Budd*, Melville] is trying, as it were with his final breath, to reveal the knowledge that has been haunting him—that these things must be so and not otherwise.

Freeman, John. *Herman Melville*. New York: Macmillan, 1926.

English poet and literary scholar John Freeman praises *Billy Budd* for what he interprets as its celebration of both legal justice and human heroism. One of the chapters, titled "*Moby-Dick* and *Billy Budd*," shows how quickly the novella has come to be considered a masterpiece just two years after it was published.

If it seems fantastic to compare *Moby-Dick* with Milton's *Paradise Lost* and assert a parallel conception in each, it will seem fantastic to say that in a shorter story, *Billy Budd*, may be found another *Paradise Regained*. Like *Moby-Dick* this late and pure survival of Melville's genius has a double interest, the interest of story and the interest of psychology. . . . Finished but a few months before the author's death and only lately published, *Billy Budd* shows the imaginative faculty still secure and powerful, after nearly forty years' supineness, and the not less striking security of Melville's inward peace.

Mid-Twentieth-Century Interpretations

Anderson, Charles Roberts. "The Genesis of *Billy Budd*." *American Literature* 12:3 (1940).

This article investigates the historical accuracy of *Billy Budd*. Anderson analyzes the narrative in terms of Melville's reference to the *Somers* mutiny of 1842, when Captain Mackenzie sentenced eighteen-year-old Philip Spencer to be hanged for plotting mutiny without any evidence of his guilt. The *Somers* affair was revived for the American public through a popular magazine article, Anderson argues further, just six months before Melville began writing *Billy Budd*. One of the most interesting sections of the article is that Anderson makes a connection between Melville's story and an account of the *Somers* mutiny by James Fenimore Cooper that vilifies Captain Mackenzie.

Two of the officers protested their innocence; Spencer acknowledged all of the charges immediately but declared the whole affair was a joke, and so to the impartial observer today it obviously was—an innocent though indiscreet boyish prank. The commander, however, fearful of a general disaffection among the crew, instructed the court to find them guilty. As a result, they were hanged from the yardarm. A naval court of inquiry, ashore, justified the action. The

American public, on the other hand, was divided in opinion, some defending Captain Mackenzie, some attacking him. But one feature is common to all the contemporary accounts of the affair: without exception their discussions turned on the analyses of the characters of the accused and the accuser. The most notable of these, and one that Melville surely saw, was a brochure of a hundred pages by Fenimore Cooper, excoriating the commander for his unmanly conduct and vigorously asserting the innocence of the midshipman. . . . [the] transfer of the role of villain from the captain to the informer and accuser may have been suggested to Melville by Cooper; for the latter, after examining all of the evidence against Spencer, dismisses it as inconclusive, since it all came from one man, adding: "upon the head of this officious lieutenant, in common with that of the commander, the blood of the executed rests."

Schiffman, Joseph. "Melville's Final Stage, Irony: A Re-Examination of *Billy Budd* Criticism." *American Literature* 22:2 (1950).

Schiffman argues that we cannot read *Billy Budd* literally. More specifically, he contends that *Billy Budd* is not Melville's acceptance that individual freedom must be sacrificed for the social good, as critics from Lewis Mumford to E. L. Grant Watson contended a few years after its initial publication in 1924, but is instead a rebellious text that must be read ironically, or as Melville's resistance to conformity. Schiffman's reading would forever change the way scholars interpreted *Billy Budd*.

These critics [who read *Billy Budd* literally], it seems to me, commit three basic mistakes in their attempt at divining Melville's final moments of thought in his story. First, they divorce *Billy Budd* from all of Melville's other works in the way that a man might search for roots in treetops. Second, they isolate Melville from the Gilded Age, the time in which Melville produced *Billy Budd*. Third, and most important, they accept at face value the words "God bless Captain Vere," forgetting that Melville is always something other than obvious. . . . Billy is an ironic figure, as is Captain Vere. Scholarly, retiring, ill at ease with people, "Starry" Vere is in command of a ship at war. . . . At heart a kind man, Vere, strange to say, makes possible the depraved Claggart's wish—the destruction of Billy. "God bless Captain Vere!" Is this not piercing irony? As innocent Billy utters these words, does not the reader gag?

Late-Twentieth-Century Interpretations

Wallace, Robert K. "*Billy Budd* and the Haymarket Hangings." *American Literature* 47 (1975).

Wallace considers one of the most intriguing questions about the publication of *Billy Budd*: how would readers have interpreted it had it been published just after it was written? Because the text was first published over thirty years after Melville's death in 1891, and because it comments on history and politics so extensively, and because Melville left nothing behind indicating his opinions on the text, many critics and readers have proposed theories regarding its relevant contexts. Wallace claims that one of the most important contexts was the Haymarket affair, during which seven men were sentenced to death for planting a bomb in Haymarket Square in Chicago. One convict committed suicide in his cell, four were hanged, and two were eventually sentenced to life in prison, even though no hard evidence actually linked them to the crime. Governor Altgeld pardoned the remaining two men, in what many saw as evidence of the group's innocence in the affair.

> Because Melville alluded to the *Somers* affair in the text of *Billy Budd*, critics have felt secure in pointing to that incident and its revival in the late 1880s as, first, the original source for Melville's story and, later, a "cogent analogue" to the story's final version. . . . Melville wrote *Billy Budd* during the years in which the nation agonized over Haymarket; the plot and themes of the final version of the novel parallel Haymarket events; the issues Melville addressed in successive versions of the novel match the issues arising from successive Haymarket developments; the Haymarket affair was responsible for the *Somers* revival and for whatever influence the latter may have had on *Billy Budd*. . . . [P]erhaps a chief reason why this connection has not previously been pointed out is that the delayed publication of *Billy Budd*—thirty-three years after Melville's death and thirty-one years after Altgeld's pardon of Fielden and Schwab—robbed not only its first readers but most critics of the context in which to appreciate its topicality.

Parker, Hershel. "The Inherently Problematical Nature of the Text." *Reading Billy Budd*. Evanston: Northwestern University Press, 1990.
    This book is a fascinating study of *Billy Budd*'s evolu-

tion from Melville's drafts to the unfinished final manuscript to the various editions of the text published in the twentieth century. After recalling the history of the manuscript between the time it was written and the time it was published, and then relating the story of its canonization and radical corrections made by Harrison Hayford and Merton M. Sealts in 1962, Parker offers a series of detailed interpretations of each chapter of *Billy Budd*. The excerpt here comes from his conclusion.

> Our task, having absorbed some of the lessons of Hayford and Sealts in their study of *Billy Budd, Sailor*, is to acknowledge the fact that when we read their text we are dealing with a work that is not quite finished, that contains a number of small contradictions, that contains clues as to the behavior of a main character, Captain Vere, which seem to lead both to favorable and to unfavorable judgments, and that contains at least one important chapter, the one on Lord Nelson, which the author might have left out of the book if he had lived to print it. The other part of our task is to acknowledge that there are limits to what we can responsibly say about such a text. We cannot and should not stop reading *Billy Budd, Sailor* as a classic work of American Literature, but we should acknowledge that we do not help our reputation as readers and do not help the reputation of the work when we act as if we can offer a complete, coherent interpretation of it.

Shaw, Peter. "The Fate of a Story." *American Scholar* 62:4 (1993).

In this article, Shaw enters the debate about whether *Billy Budd* should be taken at face value. He argues that those who read irony into the text try to escape the moral dilemma the story poses and does not solve.

> *Billy Budd*, all this to say, is not merely about England at the end of the eighteenth century. Nor is it, as some critics would have it, allusively about America in the nineteenth century, though both of these places are included in its reach. *Billy Budd* is about the tragic possibilities inherent in society's invocation of its ultimate power over life and death when faced with an external threat to its existence. If the story concerned an evil society that did not deserve to exist, or a naval officer who acted in a perverse manner, then the whole point would be lost. The society would be bad, or the military officer would be bad, but the conundrums of power in all human societies would not be at issue. As a result, the story would have little resonance.

Franklin, H. Bruce. "Billy Budd and Capital Punishment: A Tale of Three Centuries." *American Literature* 69:2 (1997).

Legal scholars have made *Billy Budd* central to discussions about judicial ethics. For almost a century, literary critics have discussed the justice or injustice of the story's resolution. In light of this, it is remarkable, Franklin argues, that none of these heated debates brought out one of the most central issues of the text: capital punishment.

> Somehow, astonishingly enough, nobody seems to have noticed that central to the story is the subject of capital punishment and its history. . . . Why have we

overlooked something so obvious? Is it because we ignore the history of capital punishment in the nineteenth century, including its profound influence on American culture? Or have we, who have been scrutinizing the story within the post–World War II culture of the second half of the twentieth century, become desensitized to the implications of the issue that were so manifest to nineteenth-century Americans? In any case, if we do contextualize *Billy Budd* within the American history of capital punishment and its bizarre outcome in New York State during the years 1886 to 1891, the story transforms before our eyes. If *Billy Budd* had been published in 1891, when Melville wrote "End of Book" on the last leaf of the manuscript, few readers at the time could have failed to understand that the debate then raging about capital punishment was central to the story, and to these readers the story's position in that debate would have appeared unequivocal and unambiguous. *Billy Budd* derives in part from the American movement against capital punishment.

Neff, D. S. " 'A Spiritual Sphere Wholly Obscure': 'Lunacy,' the *Orlando Furioso,* and 'the Incident at the Mess' in *Billy Budd*." ANQ 16:1 (2003).

The episode during which Budd spills his soup in front of Claggart has been considered one of the most opaque passages in the story. One of many critics to explore the meaning of this episode, D. S. Neff convincingly suggests a unique source: Ariosto's *Orlando Furioso*, which was published in 1848 by Wiley and Putnam, a house from which Melville frequently purchased books.

Critics have found great psychological, symbolic, and allegorical significance in "the affair of the spilled soup" in *Billy Budd*, Melville's often perplexing final novel. This affair recalls a memorable glimpse of some spilled soup in the 34th canto of Ariosto's *Orlando Furioso*, which has never been examined as a possible direct source for that fateful confrontation between Claggart and Billy. . . . If St. John, Elijah, and Enoch were the "psychologic theologians" in Melville's thoughts during the writing of *Billy Budd*, the *Orlando Furioso* would also deserve some credit for inspiring such a central theme. Ariosto's romance epic helps readers of Melville's final novel understand how Claggart's charity, Billy's words of defense, and Vere's wise lessons on unavoidable and ineradicable human weakness can be seen as resting ineffectually in a lunar valley amidst all other earthly "lost time and deeds." Even if the line between "sanity and insanity," like the line in the rainbow "where the violet tint ends and the orange tint begins," ultimately constitutes "nothing" quite "namable" for the narrator of *Billy Budd*, Astolfo's journey to the moon offers an increased understanding of, if not very much hope for a way out from, Melville's troubling "labyrinth" of human madness.

QUESTIONS FOR DISCUSSION

Why do you think Melville gives Billy Budd a speech impediment? Is he the only one who cannot speak at times? What are the effects of Budd's occasional muteness?

The narrator depicts Claggart as a villain, even comparing him to Satan. But there is also a great deal of ambiguity about his character. Just like Billy, he has no known background, and much of his reputation derives from rumor and gossip. Try thinking of the story first with Claggart as "evil," then with Claggart as a good man who is the victim of mean-spirited gossip. How does changing your perspective on Claggart change your interpretation of the story?

At one point, the narrator admits that rumors "once started on the gun decks in reference to almost anyone below the rank of a commissioned officer would, during the period assigned to this narrative, have seemed not altogether wanting in credibility." What role does gossip play in the story as a whole? If nothing of the backgrounds of hero and villain alike is known, how can the narrator so clearly assert their true natures? Without the narrator's interpretations, left only with the acts and speech of the characters, how would you read the novella differently?

Do you think what Budd did to Claggart was wrong? Why or why not?

If you were Captain Vere, what would your verdict be? What legal, moral, and spiritual issues emerge during the trial? What other options could you imagine to those he considers? Given the narrator's questions of his sanity, what do you think Melville thought of his decision?

Do you read the story literally or ironically? Why or why not?

How do you interpret the full title, *Billy Budd, Sailor (An Inside Narrative)*? Where does the narrator provide or deny the inside perspective of the story?

SUGGESTIONS FOR THE
INTERESTED READER

If you liked *Billy Budd*, you might also be interested in the following:

Moby-Dick; or, The Whale by Herman Melville (1851). A much longer narrative about adventures at sea, *Moby-Dick* is considered a literary masterpiece, one of the world's greatest novels. Also try the classic 1956 film version of the book, starring Gregory Peck as Captain Ahab.

"Benito Cereno" by Herman Melville (1855). This is a short story that evokes themes similar to those in *Billy Budd*. Based on a true story, it concerns a slave revolt at sea and considers the consequences of slavery during a crucial time in American history, when the country was on the brink of war over the issue.

Mutiny on the Bounty (DVD, VHS, 1935). Clark Gable and Charles Laughton star in this epic dramatization of the mutiny in April 1789 during which Fletcher Christian forces Captain William Bligh from the HMS *Bounty*, a British naval ship. At the Academy Awards in 1935, both Gable and Laughton were nominees for Best Actor, and the film won Best Picture. *Billy Budd* readers may find the characterization interesting: though Christian is depicted as the hero, Bligh is something of a sympathetic villain.

The Handsome Sailor by Larry Duberstein (1998). In this historical novel, Duberstein imagines what Melville experienced after publishing *Moby-Dick* in 1851 and watching his reputation as a writer dissolve, and especially what his life was like during his long silence, which built up to his composition of *Billy Budd*.

BESTSELLING ENRICHED CLASSICS

JANE EYRE
Charlotte Brontë
$4.95

WUTHERING HEIGHTS
Emily Brontë
$4.95

THE GOOD EARTH
Pearl S. Buck
$6.99

**_THE AWAKENING_ AND
SELECTED STORIES**
Kate Chopin
$4.95

**_HEART OF DARKNESS_
AND _THE SECRET SHARER_**
Joseph Conrad
$4.95

GREAT EXPECTATIONS
Charles Dickens
$4.95

A TALE OF TWO CITIES
Charles Dickens
$4.95

UNCLE TOM'S CABIN
Harriet Beecher Stowe
$5.95

16210-1

FROM POCKET BOOKS

POCKET BOOKS
A Division of Simon & Schuster

PRIDE AND PREJUDICE
Jane Austen
$4.95

OEDIPUS THE KING
Sophocles
$5.50

LES MISERABLES
Victor Hugo
$5.99

FRANKENSTEIN
Mary Shelley
$3.95

THE JUNGLE
Upton Sinclair
$5.95

**ADVENTURES OF
HUCKLEBERRY FINN**
Mark Twain
$4.95

ETHAN FROME
Edith Wharton
$4.95

THE SCARLET PIMPERNEL
Emmuska Orczy
$4.95

10210-2